YA
FICTION
NEU

Neufeld, John.

Boys lie.

$16.95

DATE			

Boys Lie

A Richard Jackson Book

Other books by John Neufeld

Boys Lie

a novel by John Neufeld

A DK INK BOOK

DK PUBLISHING, INC.

A Richard Jackson Book

DK Publishing, Inc.
95 Madison Avenue
New York, New York 10016

Visit us on the World Wide Web at http://www.dk.com

Library of Congress Cataloging-in-Publication Data
Neufeld, John.
    Boys lie / John Neufeld. — 1st ed.
        p.   cm.
    Summary: Eighth-grader Gina is targeted as easy
by some boys in her new school because of her physical
development and an incident in her past in which she was
assaulted in a public swimming pool.
    "A Richard Jackson book"—T.p. verso.
    ISBN 0-7894-2624-2
    [1. Sex—Fiction.   2. Schools—Fiction.]   I. Title.
PZ7.N4425Bo   1999   [Fic]—dc21   98-34546   CIP   AC

Book design by Annemarie Redmond.
The text of this book is set in 11 point Adobe Caslon.

Printed and bound in U.S.A.

First Edition, 1999
10   9   8   7   6   5   4   3   2   1

Boys Lie

1

From the water, if one looked up at just the right angle, the girl appeared nearly as tall as the city towers in the distance. She stood a moment without moving, her toes curled over the edge of the cement, a statue surrounded by sound: blaring radios, crying children, mothers calling, teens laughing and teasing one another.

She was encircled, it seemed, by heat waves. Some of these rose from the cement on which she stood; some wavered a few inches off the ground, like static. Clouds blocked the sun for a moment, the heat waves shimmered, and the girl lifted her arms, brushing her hands through her damp hair. Her one-piece tank suit rose with the motion and then settled again around her body as she took first one step and then a second down toward the pool.

She eased into the crowded shallow end, letting herself sink for a moment below the water's surface to drown out all the noise above her. When she stood again, smiling to be refreshed amid the heat and confusion, her suit stuck to her figure revealingly.

After a moment she let herself fall forward into the patternless waves, reaching out with both arms to breaststroke a few feet, her eyes closed against the renewed heat of the sun above.

She was perhaps thirty feet from the edge of the cement. She stood and shielded her eyes, looking back toward the friends she'd come with for an afternoon's relief from the city's surprisingly early heat wave. As her glance swept the poolside, her eyes glided over and across the figure of a lifeguard on top of his white lookout station, standing alert and strong-looking, his nose covered with zinc oxide.

Someone nearby splashed a friend. The girl seemed startled by the movement and the sudden shower. She turned to see whose hands had targeted her but realized quickly that she was merely in the wrong place at the wrong time. She ducked once more beneath the surface to cool off and on rising took another few steps toward the deeper water, where she planned to test herself. Last summer she had been able to hold her breath long enough to swim nearly the entire fifty yards of the pool's length. She imagined that with her extra year's growth and strength, she should be able to reach her goal easily.

A boy was standing in the water not far from her. She sensed his presence rather than saw it, just as she sensed his eyes, his glance, the targets of his interest. Idly she ran her hands through her hair again and took a few more steps into the deep.

The boy followed, now accompanied by another, a second shadow on the girl's radar.

She turned to face them suddenly.

Both boys halted, embarrassed to be caught staring. To cover their surprise, one boy seemed thoughtlessly to splash the other. His friend grinned and splashed back. The girl took a few steps away from them and nearly bumped into a third boy, standing as if rooted to the pool's cement bottom. Without a word to her or to his friends, if indeed they all knew one another, he swept his arm across the surface of the water, too.

The girl would have swum away then, out of range, if she had not looked into the third boy's eyes and seen there something that startled her, frightened her. By the time their eyes unlocked, a fourth and then a fifth boy were at her sides, tentatively splashing past her body at the others.

The girl smiled uneasily, looking once more at the third boy, trying to soften his stare. He did not smile back, and in a moment other boys, younger ones now, bobbed in the water no farther than arm's distance. All seemed to be fixed on the girl, their eyes bright with mischief and unspoken agreement.

The girl froze, her arms folded protectively across her chest.

As though alerted by a distant, silent signal, the water around her erupted.

At first all the girl could do was close her eyes against the chlorinated cascade hurled her way. But after a few seconds she ducked under the water for protection and tried to push her way forward, toward the deep end of the pool, out of the circle of boys. She ran into someone's legs. She stopped and stood up, just as the first hand touched her.

Startled, she was inclined to think the touch accidental. She whirled but couldn't decide to which boy the hand belonged. Without warning then she felt a second hand, a touch that was definitely not accidental.

She spun around, her fist clenched, ready to strike. But as she did, another hand from behind caught the top of her tank suit. The splashing continued; laughter seemed to be growing, sounds around her registering too loudly, too confusingly.

Suddenly she was pulled backward, under the water, by the hand that was grasping her suit at its top. She gasped. Underwater, hands came from all sides.

She fought, angry now, more angry than frightened. She batted hands and fingers away as best she could, tried to grab at them and twist, but her air was running out. She struggled to regain her stance and surfaced just as someone reached through the watery din and grabbed the front of her tank suit. In the laughter and noise of the attack, she didn't hear the suit give way.

A boy, one of the younger ones, ducked underwater then and took hold of her ankles. He yanked hard, and once more the girl found herself below the waves.

Fingers and hands and knees assaulted her. A boy's head pierced the pool's roiling surface and tried to nuzzle her. Another hand reached between her legs.

Anger turned to panic, and her vision was blurred now by more than chlorinated stinging water. She could not scream.

With what seemed a gigantic effort, the girl broke the surface, swinging out defiantly with one hand while with the other she tried to maintain her modesty. But the attack was relentless: hands pinched and prodded, groped and slid, tore and explored. The girl tried to scream, her face contorted in the ceaseless deluge.

The lifeguard, standing ever alert on his white-painted tower, a whistle on a lanyard around his neck, in his hand a battery-operated megaphone, scanned the pool and smiled to see so many people having fun.

2

Cradling her newly collected textbooks against her chest, Gina slid into a chair at the front of the classroom. Five minutes remained before homeroom began, before a teacher would enter and call the class to order.

Gina had arrived at her new school early. At her old school she had seen how difficult it was for others to enter an already quieted room, pause embarrassedly at the doorway, and then be motioned forward to the side of a teacher's desk. There, standing awkwardly and feeling foolish, the new student would be introduced.

Having slipped unnoticed through registration in the company of her mother the day before, Gina planned that she would not be singled out in any way when school actually began. She had purposely dressed down: a dark blouse tucked into her jeans and a light cotton sweater over her shoulders. Her hair was neatly combed, and the lipstick she wore was more natural than red. In her plan for the day, she had decided to utter only one necessary word: "Here."

Behind her she could hear others entering the classroom after the long summer's holiday. She could tell by listening, although she hoped to appear disinterested, that some hadn't seen one another since the previous June, while others had spent hours on a telephone or entire days together at a nearby beach. By next year, in ninth grade, she would be one of the latter. She hoped.

She busied herself, pretending to search for something

important in her purse. She imagined being watched from above by an invisible camera, the one dark small dot of still-ness in a sea of color and laughter and movement. As far as she was concerned, that was perfect.

Although she hoped that by the end of this week she would have made one or two friends, all she wanted to do in the meantime was exist, ease into her new situation as pain-lessly and quietly as possible. That was the reason, when her mother had asked why she wore a sweater over her shoul-ders since the California day was warm and fine, Gina hadn't answered honestly.

There was a sudden burst of laughter at the door be-hind her. She did not turn.

Ben Derby pushed his way through the crowd and slid into a chair near his best friend. He jammed his textbooks under his desk and looked up at Felix Moldanado, who had already assumed his usual casual slouch. Felix was smart and got good grades when he wanted to. He simply didn't want any of his teachers to take them, or him, for granted.

To acknowledge his friend's presence, Felix smiled faintly and pointed with his chin toward the front of the classroom.

Ben looked forward. He saw nothing unusual. He turned back to Felix and shrugged in puzzlement.

Felix stuck out his chin again, nodding his head three times and moving it from left to right. Ben looked and counted as directed.

What he saw was long dark hair caught in a ponytail, two hunched shoulders wrapped in a thin chocolate sweater, and the back of a chair. The girl's head did not move, did not look from side to side so that Ben couldn't see what this new presence looked like. "So?" he said quietly to Felix.

"Fox." This was said flatly, almost under Felix's breath. "You haven't seen yet."

Ben looked again and still couldn't tell whether the new girl was pretty. What he could see clearly was Jennie Johnson seated in the same row, a couple of chairs over from the new girl, Jennie turning halfway in her chair to look for him. When their eyes met, each smiled.

Ben felt his spirits rise. He reached out and lightly punched Felix's shoulder, just as other throats were cleared and chairs were shuffled a bit as the class's homeroom teacher strode forward, attendance book in hand, ready to begin taking roll.

"Got mine," he said proudly.

3

"It's hard, isn't it?"

Gina lifted her head and turned. There at her side, carrying a tray, was a girl she had seen all morning, even in the hallways as students scurried from one classroom to another for each new period and subject.

"Coming into a new school, a new situation," the girl said, putting her tray down beside Gina's.

Gina nodded and smiled just a little. "You know that, and I do. Why don't our mothers?"

"You mean you got the same sendoff I always get?" asked the girl now, sitting and taking food from her tray. " 'Just think of all the new friends you'll make'?"

"Exactly."

"I'm Jennie Johnson," said the girl then. "We have the same homeroom."

"And a lot of other classes, too," Gina replied.

"You're Gina, right? Nice name," said Jennie, unwrapping the foil from her lasagna. "So, where was home last year?"

Gina shrugged. "Back east."

"New York?"

Gina was startled.

"You have the tiniest trace of an accent," Jennie explained. "Nothing huge, mind you. Probably most kids wouldn't even notice. But I've been able to get around a bit. My dad's a computer whiz. He's always rushing off to solve someone's software problems. Sometimes he takes us with him."

Gina nodded.

After a moment of silence Jennie asked, "What's your dad do?"

"I don't know. Really."

"But why? Is he under government protection or something? I mean, I've seen movies where people do something for the government, but because of the danger this puts them in, they need new identities and new places to live secretly. Is it something like that?"

Gina laughed. "No, it's much simpler," she explained. "He left my mom five or six years ago. We just don't know where he is or what he's doing. And we try not to care."

"That must be hard."

Gina nodded.

"Hi."

Gina looked up at the same time Jennie did. There, standing across the cafeteria table from them, stood a tallish redheaded boy, his face still freckled and tanned from the summer just ending.

"Hi," Jennie said, smiling broadly. "Gina, this is Ben Derby."

Gina nodded shyly.

Ben stood blushing, shifting his weight from one leg to the other. "I was thinking of going by Dad's later. Want to come?"

"I'd love to, but I can't," Jennie answered. "Mom's suddenly looking ahead at my future. I'm supposed to go directly home, every day, no matter what. If I want to get into a good college, she says I have to concentrate on my studies. She's become very PBS."

"Well"—Ben sighed—"she's probably right."

"That's what makes me so mad," Jennie admitted.

"I guess I'll see you later then," Ben said slowly, "maybe on the weekend?"

"We can hope," Jennie allowed, looking up at her friend and grinning. Then she blew him a silent kiss.

Ben's face turned darker than his hair.

"He's nice," Gina said after he had turned to walk out of earshot.

Jennie nodded. "Um-hmm. I like him."

Gina looked closely at her new companion, at the fair brown curls, her clear complexion, her bright eyes. "Are you two a thing?"

"Oh God, no! Well, maybe, in a kind of way. I mean, we like to hang around together, that's all. We have fun."

A bell rang. They had only five minutes to finish first lunch and get to their next classes. Gina and Jennie stood up.

Gina's sweater fell from her shoulders as she turned to push her chair back under the table's edge. Instinctively she reached to grab it before it landed on the floor. When she stood straight again, she threw it back around her shoulders but not before Jennie's eyes had widened.

"Gina, you—you've got—"

It was Gina who blushed now. "I know. Don't say it."

"But that's wonderful!" Jennie exclaimed. "You'll be the

envy of every seventh grader in the place, not to mention most of us eighth graders. Ohmygod! And the boys!"

Gina quickly scanned the tables nearby. The one pair of eyes she caught belonged to a boy with dark, straight hair and a sort of wiseass grin on his face. He sat slouched at a table a few feet away, the fork in his hand tapping some mysterious rhythm, nodding his head perceptibly in time to the music he was hearing in his mind.

Gina could not hold his glance.

4

Ben got off the bus and waited a second for State Street traffic to ease so he could cross to his father's restaurant. He could already smell what was on the grill, fajitas of beef and chicken, peppers, onions, garlic bread. He approached the freshly painted adobe wall that surrounded the restaurant's patio feeling as he always did when he stopped by after school: relief, pleasure, anticipation. He liked his father.

"Ben!"

Ben stood a moment, adjusting his eyes to the interior of the first dining room. The voice had not been his father's. He frowned.

It wasn't that he didn't like Valerie. She was nice. She tried to listen to him. She pretended he was a grown-up. But she and his father had just announced their engagement.

"Hi, sweetheart!" she greeted him happily, putting an arm around Ben's shoulders before he could move away. She hugged him quickly. "So, how was it? New friends? New girls?"

Ben shrugged out of her one-armed embrace. "Is Dad here?"

"Sure he is, honey. I'll go get him."

"No, it's O.K. I'll find him."

Before Valerie could object, Ben had taken a few quick steps and rounded a corner, starting down a hallway that led past the kitchens to his father's office. He did not stop outside the door, which was slightly ajar. Instead, he grinned and pushed it open, sticking his head into the room. "Hey, Dad."

"Hi there, sport!" His father rose from behind his desk smiling, a vigorous, handsome man in his late thirties who took pride in his attire, his diet, his exercise. "Did you see Val?"

Ben nodded. "I tried to bring Jennie along, but she's being studious. I don't know what her mother has in mind for an 'or else' but I bet it's something."

"Well, good for her—Jennie's mother, I mean. This is the time, Ben. It's not too early to start looking down the road. You'll have a lot of important decisions to make in the next few years."

"Yeah," Ben agreed. "I know. Still and all, on the first day of school?"

His father held up both hands, palms out. "Hey, if I were the kind of father I'd like to be, I'd be on your case, too."

"Sure, but sensible."

"It's a tough line to walk, kiddo, let me tell you. Especially as you all get older."

"Well, you two! Every time I turn around you're 'bonding.' " Valerie stood with her hands on her hips just inside the office.

Ben's dad grinned broadly and crossed to her side, putting his arm around her waist. He brought her body in toward his own for a second. "What's up, honey? Got a problem?"

"No," Valerie replied with a toss of her blond hair. "I just missed you both. Besides, when you're off huddling like this . . . I may be paranoid, but I always think you're talking about me."

"You should be so lucky!" Ben's father laughed and kissed her cheek quickly.

Ben was just a little embarrassed. Not that his father didn't deserve to have fun, to find a pretty woman and have a relationship. Last year he and Ben had talked about exactly this sort of thing. Then, because there was no particular woman immediately on the horizon, it was easy for Ben to be understanding and agreeable.

"You want to stick around and have dinner?" his dad asked.

"Well, I don't know. I've got to walk Baines and feed Nigel and all."

"They can hold out for a little while, I bet. The only thing is, Ben, Val and I have to leave you. We've got to get out to a few furniture stores before they close. A new house is wonderful, but we still need a lot of stuff."

Ben nodded, unable to stop himself from thinking that they could have suggested he come with them.

"Listen," his father continued, "I can ask Irene to set you up here before she leaves. Or I could call your grandmother to come join you. She'd love that."

Normally, Ben was wild about his grandmother's company. She had a great deep voice, she still smoked no matter what anyone read or said, and she liked a drink from time to time so that talking with her, listening to her, was really fun.

Irene was his father's accountant and bookkeeper, and Felix's mother. She had worked for his father ever since Ben could recall. Everything good in her son came down in a direct line from her.

But his father's suggestions were, Ben saw immediately, less off-the-cuff great ideas than offerings to appease his own guilt at spending less and less time with his son.

"Well, maybe I just better head home." On the tip of Ben's tongue was the line "Three's a crowd." He kept his mouth shut.

5

Gina stood at her bedroom window, looking out, down a slight hill. She knew the beach was to her right, just out of sight. So, of course, was the ocean. Water. She shuddered and then straightened her spine. She would get over all that. She had to. Because compared with how she and her mother lived in New York, this was paradise.

From her window Gina could see parts of downtown Santa Barbara and the mountains in the distance, dotted with increasingly expensive houses as roads curved and wound up toward the top of a hill that separated Santa Barbara from a place called Montecito. There were tall, singular trees on these hillsides, the sorts of trees one saw in dubbed foreign movies on television.

She turned when she heard a door close behind her in the house. "I'm so sorry, sweetheart," her mother said breathlessly, coming directly into Gina's room. "I tried to get away early but this being my first day and all, it just wasn't to be."

Gina nodded understandingly. At the same moment she and her mother spoke, asking the same question: "So, how was it?"

Together they laughed. Gina's mother threw her handbag on one of the twin beds in the room and sat on the other. "Not so bad," she admitted. "The staff seems friendly. Doctors are doctors. You know. Busy, cool. My hope is that when I pass the California test, things will brighten up a bit. Right now I would guess people are sort of suspicious, wondering if I'm up-to-date or if we ever heard of computers back in New York. In a way, I'm on probation. I can handle it." She paused. "But wait! How'd you get home?"

Gina grinned. "A nice kid and his mother dropped me off. They live behind us somewhere, maybe a mile or so."

"And this kid's name is?"

"MacNulty."

"What's his first name?"

"MacNulty. MacNulty Love."

Gina's mother smiled. "Are they black?"

Gina shook her head. "Nope, just odd. A little, I mean. Nothing threatening. Mac's in my class, sort of an all-American type: not too bright but not stupid, not pushy but also not that shy. I don't know. He's just a kid."

"Gee, the way things are these days, being just a kid is tough."

"You're telling the wrong girl," Gina said with a little laugh. "What I mean is, he's got two parents."

Gina's mother laughed in turn. "No! Well, so do you."

"I mean, living in the same house, getting along."

"Oh, in that case, he is stranger than you described."

"He is not!"

"What is this? Love at first sight?"

"Hardly. Mac's just a nice boy, period. His mother's nice. You'd like her."

Gina's mother leaned back on the bed and drew up her legs. "Think we've landed on both feet?"

Gina shrugged. "Who knows? I hope so. It's a little early yet."

"We've been very lucky, you know," her mother said. "To be able to get out, away from all that. To have found a job, a nice house to rent. A cheap car. God, it's been years since I've even thought about driving."

"It seems like a nice town, though. I'm glad we came."

"Sweetheart, I couldn't let you grow up in the middle of all that trash."

Gina smiled a little. "I imagine there's some of that around here, too."

Gina's mother stood up from the bed and took the two steps across Gina's bedroom to embrace her. "It's going to be fine. You'll see. You're going to be fine."

"As old Mrs. Goldstein used to say, 'From your lips to God's ear.' "

6

"Feeding time at the zoo over?" Felix asked Ben on the telephone an hour later.

"Yeah. What's up?"

"Not a lot. Hanging out. You want to come down?"

Ben thought a moment. He didn't know when his father and Valerie were returning. His aunt Eileen, whose presence he missed, had settled into her new condo out near the Mirador. His sheltie, Baines, had been walked and fed; Nigel, his marmalade and white cat, had been fed and scratched and groomed. Maybe Felix's mom was cooking. "Sure," he decided. "I'll be there in fifteen minutes."

He closed up the house and pulled out his bicycle from the garage. The sun still hung above the ocean in the distance. He wouldn't need his lights till later. He could almost glide down to Felix's.

Except that, in his new neighborhood, the roads weren't straight and simple. A couple of times on his bike Ben had had to hug a retaining wall in front of someone's house in order not to be creamed by a car racing up the hills at full speed, rounding corners wildly, swinging from the center of the road to its limits.

Ben liked the new neighborhood. It was certainly prettier than his old one, and its houses were nicer, too: bigger, more interesting because of the slope of the hills they stood on. Many had views of downtown Santa Barbara; some, farther up the hill, had views reaching to the ocean. But it wasn't quite as friendly as his old neighborhood. Ben didn't know his neighbors yet. Getting around town was more difficult, too, taking more time, more planning. In the old days, just a year before, he had been able to mount his bike and be at Felix's in eight minutes.

He pulled into the driveway and rested his bike against the house. He thought a moment about locking it and then decided not to. Santa Barbara wasn't different from other towns, he knew. Things disappeared when you least expected. On the other hand, forewarned was forearmed, and Ben decided he would just—every so often—walk by a front window and look out.

He smiled as he mounted the three steps up to Felix's front door; he could already smell sautéing onions. He'd made a good guess.

So, apparently, had Felix's brother and two sisters, whose cars—in one state of disrepair or another—were parked either at curbside or behind the house.

Felix pulled open the front door, grinning a little wickedly. "So," he teased, "what do you think of the air down here?"

Ben shrugged. "Not bad. A little smoggy. Hey, give it a rest. The move wasn't my idea."

Felix nodded. "Come on in."

Ben followed Felix into a family room where a TV was on with the early news. Eddie Phipps lay across a couch, reaching down into a bowl of nachos, stuffing his face. As usual. He waved lazily at Ben. "Hi," Ben said. Eddie Phipps was not Ben's idea of a good friend.

"We were just ventilating," Felix said.

"About what?"

"The new girl."

Ben nodded. "What about her?" he asked innocently.

"She's got a huge pair," Eddie announced with a full mouth. Ben noticed his sneakers had left streaks on the couch. What a slob!

"If you put every other girl's assets together," Felix estimated, "you'd still come up short of what she's got."

Ben couldn't think of anything to say that didn't sound stupid. He could hear Irene's voice from the kitchen at the back of the house.

"That's a bank I'd like to break," Eddie said with a laugh.

"She's not just another girl," Felix said, flopping down into a chair and crossing his ankles as he folded his arms across his chest. He nodded, trying to look wise.

"What are you talking about?" Ben asked. "I talked to her. She seems normal enough."

Felix shook his head and closed his eyes. Ben recognized the expression: Hey, I've got this knocked.

"Felix thinks she's got a secret," Eddie announced.

"You do? What kind?"

Felix shrugged smugly. "But I tell you one thing, she knows."

"Knows what?" Ben asked.

"Oh, come on!" Eddie sat up and peeled his legs off the couch. "Hey, Ben, come on. We're talking sex here."

"Oh."

Felix laughed a little. Ben was annoyed. Why Felix let this creep hang around was more than he could imagine.

"I'm not saying she's done it," Felix added after a moment of thought. "Just that she knows about it. Knows how, when, why."

"Hey, so does everybody else," Ben said then. "I mean, it's not like we haven't all figured it out by now."

"That's not what I mean," Felix explained. "This girl's got perfume, you know what I mean?"

"No," Ben replied.

"There's just something about her," Felix went on. "Some people have a sort of thing about them. It's not something they're even aware of. It's what makes movie stars movie stars. Get it?"

"Not yet," Ben said.

"Look, Ben . . ." Eddie Phipps stood up. "Some people have what our parents call sex appeal. I'd just call it a physiological aura."

"You would?" Felix asked, laughing. "You sound just like your folks!"

Eddie blushed. "Don't rub it in," he warned. "You know what I mean."

"You mean she sends out signals?" Ben guessed.

"Exactly!" Eddie swung his arms in agreement and pleasure. "Hey, she may not even be aware of it."

"She's aware," Felix said darkly.

"How do you know?" Eddie asked.

But before Felix could answer, the three heard a car horn outside at the curb.

"Nuts!" Eddie grumbled.

Ben took a couple of steps toward the front windows to look out into the street. Idling there, its driver unidentified, was one of the Phippses' cars, the Mercedes.

"Your chariot," Felix said.

"I know, I know," Eddie groaned. "I hate this. When I'm sixteen, I'm on my own."

"You wish. You'd have to leave town, join the navy or something."

Eddie had started toward the front door. He turned and stopped, grinning. "Not until I get my degree in studism!"

Felix laughed exaggeratedly and fell to the floor. "Not with this girl! She's way ahead of you!"

"Yeah, well, we'll see, won't we?" Eddie challenged, his hand on the doorknob. To emphasize his determination, he flexed the muscle in his right arm.

Felix rolled onto his side. Then he stopped laughing suddenly and stood up. "I'll tell you something, Eddie, old man. This girl is so far beyond you, you're not even on her radar. Besides, if I'm right and she's with the program already, the last thing she needs is a muscle-bound trust fund. What she needs is smooth, man."

Eddie gave Felix the finger and departed.

"What makes you so sure?" Ben asked then, after glancing quickly once again out the window to make sure his bike was where he had left it.

"Sure of what?"

"That she's 'with the program.' As far as I know, you can't really tell these things just by looking, anyway."

23

"How about not *looking?*" Felix suggested meaningfully.

"What do you mean?"

"Well, Benny, I already gave her a look. I shot her my patented 'Honey, you don't know how lucky you can get.' "

"And?"

"And! And! Well, for one thing, she knew exactly what I meant. And for another, she turned away. She knows what the look means and she's afraid."

"Maybe it was just too weird for her."

"Trust me, Benny, old son, she knows that look. She's seen it before. She knows about"—and here Felix inhaled deeply and spoke in a whisper—"fate."

"Fate maybe, but that doesn't mean she knows about sex."

"It's my guess, Watson, that she not only knows about it, she wants it."

"Bananas."

"Bananas right back. And I'll promise you one thing, it sure as hell isn't going to be silver-plated Eddie Phipps who gets there first."

7

Eddie was silent as his mother drove toward the hills, away from Felix's house on Arrellaga Street. Their route would take them up and into the section of Santa Barbara called the Riviera because of its views of downtown and the harbor. The streets were narrow and twisting, and it was easy to get lost.

But not for Eddie's mother, who looked over inquiringly at her son as she signaled a right turn onto Santa Barbara Street, then a left onto Anapamu.

"Bad day?" she asked quietly, barely audible above the smooth workings of the engine beneath her hood.

"Can I say something?" Eddie asked, pouting a little.

"Of course."

"Don't take this the wrong way, O.K.?"

His mother smiled. "Go ahead."

Eddie was tempted to turn in his seat to look at his mother. He didn't. "You and Dad . . ." he began.

"Yes?"

"Well, do you think . . . I know this sounds funny, but it's important. Do you think you could sort of talk in plain English when you're around me?"

"What do you mean?" asked his mother. "We speak perfectly."

"That's the trouble," Eddie argued, now turning to glare. "You speak *so* well, you use *such* big words."

"You understand them well enough, dear."

"I know I do. But—but it's catching. You know what I mean?"

"No, I don't, Edward."

He inhaled and tried again. "What I mean is that I can't help picking things up, you know? I mean, I hear you and Dad, and the words you use are words I understand. Then, when I'm with my friends, those words come slipping out. It's embarrassing. People think I'm showing off."

"Edward, how could your friends be offended by good English?"

"They're not," Eddie said quickly. "They just think I'm teasing them or something, using words like—like 'physiological' or—or 'psychological.' "

"None of your friends knows those words?"

"Of course they do, but . . . I don't know, if they were saying something that needed that word, like 'psychological,' they'd use 'crazy' maybe, or 'weird,' or—I don't know—'scientific.' "

His mother frowned as she guided the car into Montecito. "Edward, your father and I want you to be able to speak well, to read well, to recognize and use your vocabulary so that next year, when you head east, you will feel confident of your abilities."

"That's another thing!" Eddie nearly shouted. "Who made the decision about going east? I don't want to go away to school. My friends are here. The people I know. I don't want to leave Santa Barbara. Everything I have is here."

His mother smiled again. "What you learn here is something that you can carry always with you. We want you

26

to have the tools to prosper as you get older. I love Santa Barbara, too. But you'll be better prepared for life if you get a broader, a deeper education than is available in this vicinity."

"There! That's exactly what I was talking about!"

"What?"

"This 'vicinity.' Why not just say 'here' or 'in town' or something simple? I pick up these things and then forget how they sound until they come out. That's exactly what I mean."

"You're embarrassed to use words of more than two syllables?"

"No! I'm embarrassed when I use your words of more than two syllables!"

His mother signaled a left-hand turn, into the hills above Coast Village Road. "You know, dear, your father and I moved up here to make certain you would have the healthiest surroundings, and the safest. We are happy to invest everything we have to make sure our only child fosters his talents. I don't see a good vocabulary as something shameful. As a matter of fact, I don't see anything shameful at all in the way we have raised you."

Eddie decided there was little profit in continuing this discussion. He looked out at the countryside, which was growing more barren as they scaled their hillside, and concentrated on something entirely different, something that always calmed him down. He needed to work on his traps and deltoids that day.

Gina's mother pulled her car to a slow stop at the curb outside Gina's school. Her uniform, cap, and white shoes lay in a neat pile on the backseat.

"I'll try to be here when you get out," she told her daughter. "I'm just not in a position to slip away yet."

"I know, Mom," Gina said. "Not to worry."

She opened the passenger door and stepped onto the grass. But rather than close the door behind her and enter school, Gina stooped back into the car's cab quickly. "That's the Loves' car over there." She pointed. "That's Mac's mother."

"Really?" her mother said as she switched off the ignition.

"What are you doing?" Gina asked.

Her mother was already out of the car and walking toward the Loves.

Gina trailed quickly. "Mom!"

"I want to thank her for yesterday," Gina's mother explained. "And also, you know, meet her. We need all the friends we can find."

Gina blushed quickly. There was nothing she could do. Her mother had "theories," and a current and favorite one was that the responsibility for getting along in any new town rested on herself. She had explained this to Gina. After all, she said, they had traveled all across the country. Thank goodness her older brother, Robert, had been able to find not just a spot at the hospital but also a reasonable rental not too far from it. But he lived in New Jersey.

Therefore, as Gina's mother enjoyed concluding, the theory was simple. Every time you met a new person, you reached out. You had coffee or maybe a dinner. Then, when that person responded in kind and perhaps invited you into her home, it was up to you to make the most of the moment. Especially if there were other guests. With just one friend in a town, Gina's mother said, you could progress from that single contact and select others as you went along. Soon enough you might even be a "presence in your new community."

Gina stood silently behind as her mother introduced herself to Mrs. Love who was, just as she had been the day before, as pleasant and polite as possible. After a few seconds Gina edged away from the chatting pair and started toward school. Adults did need more than only their children for companionship.

Gina reasoned as she pulled open the school's door that she needed more than adults. MacNulty Love, Jennie Johnson . . . and her friend, Ben something.

9

"We're going out to Hendry's Beach on Saturday," Jennie announced happily to Gina. "Want to come? My mom's driving."

Fighting her instinctive reaction, Gina hedged. "Who else is going to go?"

Jennie shrugged. "Ben usually rides his bike out. Sometimes with Felix. Mac Love may come, too. Listen, it's a lot better than hanging around the mall."

"I don't know." Gina was struggling. "Since we've been out here, I hardly get to see my mom. I think she has plans for us."

"Both days?" Jennie asked brightly. "You could spend Sunday with her."

Gina felt trapped. "What's the forecast?" she asked, hoping against hope for an early autumn storm.

"Those guys can't tell us what's happening outside now," Jennie reported. "You ever see any weatherman walk to the window, look out, and say, 'Hey, it's raining'?"

Gina smiled, just a little. "Well, I'd have to check with Mom."

"It'll be fun. I bet you haven't been out there, have you?"

Gina shook her head.

"It's really beautiful. There's a great beach for walking and running, and restaurants. And cliffs. It's everybody's favorite place. Hey. Maybe your mom would like to come along, too. That would mean company for my mother, and I know she'd like that."

There had to be a way out of this. Gina gave Jennie a falsely large smile. "I'll talk to Mom. I promise. It sounds great!"

A bell sounded in the hallway.

MacNulty Love came half running through the milling students. Gina saw him catch sight of her out of the corner of his eye. He looked as if he wanted to stop, but instead he kept scurrying to his class, his face slightly more red than the exertion of worrying whether or not he might be late ordinarily caused.

10

"Sounds like fun," Gina's mother said eagerly as they dried their few dinner dishes. "I haven't met your friend Jennie's mother yet. I'd like to."

"But don't you think that—"

"Really, Gina, this is exactly what I've been talking about. The chance to meet people, make new friends."

Gina turned away from the sinkboard and leaned against it. There was nothing to do but admit her fears. "I don't want to go to the beach."

Her mother did not reply immediately. Rather, she reached across to turn off the flowing hot water and then slowly, methodically, dried her hands on her apron. She, too, turned to lean against the sinkboard. "Is it the water?" she asked quietly.

"Of course it's the water!" Gina shouted. "What is a beach except next to water?"

"Darling, you don't have to go in, you know. Many people never stick a toe in, and they think they're having a wonderful time."

Gina felt on the verge of shouting that her mother didn't understand, but she stopped. Her mother did understand.

"The thing is," Gina said, her voice low, "the other kids will probably be in bathing suits and shorts and what all. I mean, a beach is for swimming. How can I get out of that?"

Her mother smiled. "Easy. Say you don't know how to swim."

"Sure. And then someone will offer to teach me, just in the shallow part."

"You're making this more daunting than it is, Gina. First of all, you don't have to swim. You can always come to me and I'll be the villain. I'll make an excuse or find a reason. Secondly, these are friends you'll be with, not strangers. And finally, sweetheart, I'll be right there."

Gina listened and tried not to be convinced.

"I wasn't with you before," her mother went on. "I'll always regret that."

"It wasn't your fault," Gina said almost in a whisper. "It wasn't mine, either."

Gina's mother squeezed her daughter's shoulders warmly. "That's exactly what you should remember. What the therapist told you. It wasn't your fault. You did nothing that led those boys to do what they did. You're a beautiful, bright young woman who got caught in a moment of unspeakable crudity. And afterward, darling, you're still the same beautiful, bright young woman you were. Frightened, of course. Careful. Wiser."

Gina's mouth twisted slightly. "You think the kids out here are wiser, too?"

Her mother laughed gently. "Probably not. But remember, Gina, you are."

11

All week, before the coming Saturday at the beach, Gina was tempted to open her journal.

She hadn't wanted to keep one, or even start it. The idea had been her therapist's. They had shared what she had written—that is, those parts Gina wanted to share. They had relived the terrifying confusion and assault at the swimming pool. Together they had examined Gina's every action, every gesture. There was nothing evident to either of them that had precipitated the attack, certainly nothing that Gina had knowingly done.

What had happened wasn't her fault, and Gina knew this. If she had known the boys at the pool, she would have done something. What, she wasn't certain, even now. But she wouldn't have done nothing. Maybe she'd have grabbed the youngest kid and beaten the daylights out of him.

But the boys had disappeared almost as quickly as they had gathered around her. They had seemed simply to melt into the water, like ripples or waves, diving beneath the surface and not coming up for air until they were well beyond a distance that would establish their guilt.

She had been left, standing stunned, in shock, the water around her calming ever so slowly. She was clutching the front of her tank top. Tears silently rolled down her cheeks toward the pool. She had finally turned, her eyes once more passing the lifeguard atop his tower. He stood as before, confident, bronzed and zinced, his eyes roaming over the pool's surface. How could he have missed what had happened to her? What the hell good was he?

Shamed and still trembling, Gina had left the pool, not stopping by her friends on their towels with their radio blaring more of the Top Ten. She would have been too embarrassed to tell them anything.

Gina was so angry and ashamed that she skipped a shower at the pool and dressed quickly instead, half of her not even dry. She slipped out of the changing room, pushed through the turnstile and ran out onto the street. She ran all the way home.

There, finally, she stood beneath cleansing hot water. She knew that the boys at the pool wouldn't feel guilty about what they had done. Why should they? They were kids, boys, and all they had done was grab and grope someone who hadn't been expecting it. They probably thought of it as an adventure, fun. Something to brag about later among themselves.

The really troubling, secret thing that traveled with Gina wherever she went afterward was why they had chosen her. There were girls in the water who were bigger and prettier. What kinds of signals had she sent out? She had only wanted to cool off, to get away from the city's heat. She had been there with friends from school, other girls who sat on the cement poolside and sunned themselves, applied sunscreen, giggled and stared and pointed at older boys nearby. A radio had been playing. Or a tape deck. A boom box, even though that was against pool rules.

There were many mothers of younger children nearby,

too. All busy chatting and diapering and drying. How could no one have seen what was happening to her?

When she thought about these things, she shuddered. She imagined she could still feel the hands and knees and arms that came at her in the fury of the splashing. She couldn't see. She couldn't breathe. She couldn't fight back. Her swimming suit was hanging on her only by the grace of God. What could she have done?

And what, she wondered as Saturday approached, could be expected in Santa Barbara, nearly three thousand miles away from that awful initiation?

She was going to a beach with her mother. She didn't doubt that boys were boys and if she gave them a chance, they would think of some way to get to her. But they would do the same to any girl who unsuspectingly gave them a chance to show how strong and nervy they were at her expense.

On Friday night Gina tossed in her bed, unable to relax. The pictures in her mind were too vivid for rest. She tried to calm herself, to repeat special words of encouragement into the shadows above her bed. She thought of her new friends from school, of their mothers who would be nearby. At last, well after midnight, Gina decided that maybe by anticipating trouble, she was inviting it. She would never be able to guess from which direction it might come.

This thought caught her. She lay absolutely still, eyes open, staring at the ceiling over her head.

What had happened once before, just a few months earlier, couldn't happen all over again, exactly as it had. She was being hysterical even to imagine it. She was a bright, confident young woman who was growing taller day by day. Her eyes had been opened and were open, still. Her mother was right. She was wiser, more alert.

After another moment Gina smiled to herself. She would be safe. She would be on the lookout, and she would be safe.

12

Gina woke early. She lay in bed without moving, listening, hoping against hope to hear raindrops against her bedroom window.

She slid out of bed and reached to pull open the curtains just slightly. Fog!

She sighed happily. No one went to the beach when the sun was hidden.

She remembered the fear she had managed to conquer before falling asleep. Despite her relief at seeing the weather, it was still with her, filling her slowly. She felt weighed down by it.

God, what was the matter with her? All she had to do was stay alert and pretend. It was that simple.

She could pretend to be disappointed, but only after she had pretended to be enthusiastic.

She showered and dressed: plaid shorts, sneakers, and a sweatshirt. She began her day of pretense by seeming to bounce from her room and run into the kitchen where her mother was already up and preparing breakfast, as well as sandwiches to take to the beach.

Even as her mother greeted her, Gina could see water dripping from leaves outside. "What's the forecast?" she asked brightly.

Her mother shook her head. "I don't know. But I do know that no one said anything about rain last night on television. Chances are this will all burn off."

"Oh, no," Gina argued. "It's much too damp. And you can't even begin to see a break in the clouds."

The telephone rang, startling both of them.

"Hello?"

"Hi, this is Jennie's mom, Sally Johnson."

"Oh, hi. Just a sec." Gina handed the phone to her mother. "Sally Johnson."

"The day doesn't seem very cooperative, does it?" said her mother as she walked to a window and looked over their small backyard. She stood listening. "Really? By noon? I mean, you're right, we're new out here. But I can hardly imagine that—"

Gina's mother nodded at what she was hearing. "Well, if you really think . . ." She said. "You're the expert, Sally. If you say it'll clear, I'll believe you. Eleven-thirty? I guess we can wait that long. See you then. Bye."

As she handed the receiver back to Gina, her mother smiled. "Apparently, despite everything you or I know about the weather, all signals are 'Go.' "

Gina's shoulders started to sag but she pulled herself upright again quickly. "Well, we can only hope."

13

MacNulty Love's jeans and jacket were damp from the fog, but his spirits were high. He knew the sun would be shining by noon.

Mac stopped in the parking lot, straddling his bike. He loved Hendry's Beach. He often came here alone, to walk the strands and climb rocks, and to think. Mac Love always had a lot to think about. Sometimes it was schoolwork. At other times he thought about his family, how lucky he was to be part of it. Once in a while, he had a real daydream about the future, his future.

When his father's friends asked him, as they did often, what it was he wanted to be when he grew up, he never knew what to say. Things didn't stay the same, he knew. Sometimes he thought big; sometimes he thought modestly. How did he know what was coming? He wasn't even sure where his talents lay. Still, one had to give answers to grown-ups. That's what was unfair.

So was the fact that, at least for now, Mac Love was shorter than most of his classmates. Not by much, he told himself, but just enough to feel always somehow younger, babied. Sometimes someone would tease him about being stunted and accuse him of smoking cigarettes on the sly. He would laugh and josh right back, but he still felt the sting.

His father counseled him to be patient. After all, he himself was more than six feet tall, and Mac's mother was a good five feet seven. Sometimes hormones kicked in late, said his father. Be patient. Don't despair. And in the meantime, learn how to do things other kids can't.

Which Mac thought was good advice. So, when he could, and when he was alone, he came out to the beach and ran and ran until he was breathless and reeling. His narrow frame offered little resistance to winds or rain, and he seemed, as he ran, to be slipping through elements that larger kids would have trouble with.

And he was fast. Running on the sand, whether it was wet and tamped down or warm and loose, was a great conditioner. He felt strong and swift and imagined himself in high school leading the boys' cross-country team to the state championship.

He also spent a lot of time imagining himself in love. Often he would think about this without a particular girl in mind. Lately, though, he had been considering a real person. He would never tell anyone of this dream or who the girl was. It gave him a secret pleasure to think about her, to imagine holding her hand, walking along the water's edge, maybe even kissing her.

The other guys in his class talked big about what they knew, how far they got, how hot for their bods some girls were.

Mac thought this was plain make-believe. And not good manners—another reason why he would never confide in anyone about the girl he now saw walking down to the beach in a group of other people, some adults, some children.

Mac blushed just to see her.

14

Despite the fog, which really was beginning to thin out, there were clumps of people spread out on the sand already. Gina focused on these people, rather than on the broad, murmuring expanse behind them. She imagined she knew what that looked like.

Mrs. Johnson and Gina's mother both had packed coolers full of soft drinks and sandwiches and fruit. There were quilts and blankets on which to sit, and Jennie's ten-year-old sister, Marge, immediately picked up one of these and, at the edge of the parking lot, kicked off her shoes to walk toward the sand.

There was a restaurant nearby and cliffs to the north—she thought it was north, anyway. The beach looked as California beaches were supposed to, according to the ads she'd seen on television. Everything but heavy surf.

For finally she had had to look at the enemy squarely.

It was brown!

It was huge, of course. And quiet. Flat. The little rollers that broke upon the sand hardly made a sound. But it wasn't blue. Why not?

Gina walked carefully across the sand, trying to keep it from getting into her sneakers. She realized that in her thirteen years in New York she had never seen the ocean.

She stopped, watching the others set up their little picnic site. Momentarily she felt as though she were asleep and everything she saw were a dream.

There were suddenly too many new things in her life. Not just the move from coast to coast, but the way of life in California that was so different from what she had known. Everyone did everything by car. No subways; few buses. She imagined there were apartment buildings, but none that would look the way they did back east. People lived in real houses, separate and detached from one another. There were lawns and driveways and gardens and trees unlike any she had ever seen.

"Hey!" Jennie called, waving at her.

Startled from her reverie, Gina waved back and turned to join the others. Idly she wondered if what she was living in now was called suburbia. Was suburbia a place or what people called a lifestyle?

The sand was warming as the mist disappeared. And as the sun shone clearly for the first time that day, Gina sat on a blanket, feeling a little foolish for having dreaded this invitation.

Jennie was peeling off her sweater. "In ten seconds," she told Gina, "you'll be sorry you have that sweatshirt on."

"I'll wait," Gina said. "Besides, who wants to get skin cancer?"

"Here's sunscreen," her mother offered, holding out a container with "15" printed on its side.

Gina took it and uncapped the tube. She put a little on her fingers and daintily began to smooth the cream onto her face.

"Oh, good! Company!" Jennie pointed.

Loping down from the parking lot were Ben Derby and

Felix Moldanado. Beyond them, parking his bike, was Mac Love.

Gina had forgotten about boys joining the picnic. Felix was the boy in the cafeteria with whom she had locked eyes.

Although the sun was warming now, she felt a sudden chill.

15

Plastic carryalls were opened, napkins handed around, aluminum packets unfolded.

The sun was stronger now. Gina almost wished she hadn't worn her sweatshirt. Almost, but not quite. She did kick off her sneakers and, having eaten as quickly as the others in her group, she felt positively blessed. She liked Jennie and her mother; she knew she was safe with her own mother nearby. And the boys weren't too loud. There was a lot of laughter at their new teachers' expenses, though both her own mother and Jennie's tried to discourage this.

Within an hour people had settled down to bask, faces turned upward, sunscreen applied.

After a time Gina leaned up on her elbows to look at the ocean. She saw Ben Derby and Jennie walking slowly along the line of rollers that still seemed almost bathtub size.

"Want to swim?"

Gina was startled by the question, and tense immediately when she realized who had addressed her.

She shook her head. "It's too soon after lunch," she dodged.

"That's just, like, a worried parent's warning," Felix argued gently. "I don't think there's anything to it."

"Well," Gina said, "if all the food you eat goes directly to your stomach, and then you hit cold water, it seems to me you really could get cramps. Or something."

Felix nodded his head wisely, not deterred. "A walk is good for digestion," he offered.

Wheels were spinning in Gina's head. There was no good reason to fear this boy. And there was no reason not to get up and stroll around a bit with him. It didn't mean anything.

Better to keep danger in plain sight.

"Sure," she agreed suddenly, unfolding her legs and stepping off the blanket. Felix rose, too, and together, but not touching, they began to walk toward the water.

Mac Love watched silently from his blanket.

Jennie waved at Gina and Felix, beckoning them toward the ocean's edge.

"How does this compare to where you lived back east?" Jennie enthused as the quartet met just a few inches above the waterline.

"It's bigger than I imagined," Gina said a little shyly. "I never went to the beach back there. And the color isn't what I thought it would be. Where's the blue, blue of the sea?"

"Wait," Ben suggested. "Later, when the light changes, so does the color of the water. Also, the sand gets roiled sometimes overnight. Then it settles. When it does, it gets clearer, like down at Carpinteria, where it's almost always clear and blue. They've got a great beach there, and surfing."

"That's another thing I don't know much about," Gina said. "Surfing."

"Yeah, but I bet there are lots of others things you do know about," Felix gambled.

Gina gave him a wary look and ignored the comment.

The four had ambled slowly along the beachfront until

they came to a section of the sand where a lot of small children and their mothers were playing and wading in the water.

Without warning, Jennie folded her legs and plumped down onto the wet sand. Waves washed her feet lightly. "In another few weeks it'll be too cold to do this," Jennie said as Ben sat beside her. "Come on, Gina. Looking at the ocean's fine, but you've got to be able to tell your friends at home you actually went in."

"Though this really isn't swimming," Ben added.

"It will still count," Jennie said, reaching up to take Gina's hand and pulling.

Gina stood a moment, resisting, and then common sense and quick reasoning allowed her to sit beside Jennie in the Pacific. She laughed a little as the first waves curled around her feet, as they rose slightly to her knees.

Felix still stood, his arms crossed over his chest, watching Gina.

A little boy, no more than three or four, ran past them, splattering them all with water. Within seconds, his mother also ran past, although at a slower gait, saying, "I'm sorry about that."

Jennie and Ben laughed good-naturedly. Gina breathed in deeply and tried to smile.

There were little kids all around, being scooped up by mothers or older sisters, being carried from the water back up the sand toward their own temporary encampments. In the air were the delighted cries of other children splashing about, running away, squatting down to play in the sand.

In fact, when Gina looked over her shoulder, what

seemed to be the entire population of a day-care center or camp was approaching the water behind her and her friends, the children pulling on adult hands and doing everything they could to break away to run into the waves. As the first trio of kids escaped adult supervision and hit the water, both Jennie and Ben laughed. "God, remember when we were that young?" Jennie asked of no one in particular.

Gina looked at the children and smiled without meaning to. They were so cute and so small. And harmless.

"Here comes another busload," Felix said, still standing above the others. "I'm out of here."

Gina, Jennie, and Ben didn't even look around at him. The swarm of children that now seemed to move in and out with the waves was in front of them, to both sides.

It was fun to remember being a child. Gina sat next to Jennie, her shorts wet from the surf. She was smiling into the sun, her eyes closed.

Suddenly she noticed that the voices of the children playing around her had somehow grown sharper, louder. She opened her eyes to see why this might be, but then she realized that the colors of everything around her, too, had heightened, grown brighter, even garish. Without understanding why, she began to feel off-balance, edgy, disturbed.

16

A cute little four-year-old with a bowl haircut stopped running almost directly in front of Gina. Without giving any indication of why, he began suddenly to splash the three of them.

"Hey, kid! Cut it out!" Ben shouted at him, beginning to get to his knees.

"What's he doing?" asked Jennie as she shielded her face from the water.

"Hey, stop it!" Ben shouted again, now standing and starting to move toward the child.

But the boy seemed fearless, holding his ground, his fat little arms windmilling at water level.

From nearby came a horrible high-pitched shriek.

Jennie and Ben turned immediately. Gina was screaming at the top of her lungs, her arms covering her head, bent nearly double on the sand. There were no words in her cry, just fear and desperation. The sound she uttered continued and continued, grew louder and more shrill until it reached a pitch of hysteria.

Jennie knelt and tried to cradle Gina in her arms. But Gina was beyond calming, beyond control. Her eyes were squeezed tightly shut and her mouth was wide open, the unnerving treble sound issuing from it unceasingly. She was shaking violently.

Gina's outburst had cleared the area around her on the sand after a few seconds. Even the little four-year-old splasher was frightened by what he had done, and had run off.

Jennie looked imploringly up at Ben. He looked back up at the campsite where their group had lunched happily just an hour before.

He saw Gina's mother running hell for leather toward them.

By the time she reached her daughter's side and knelt to hold her, Gina was staring at the sea in front of her, her mouth still agape and her screaming no less intense.

With a gigantic effort, her mother managed to slip an arm beneath Gina's knees, the other around her back and under her shoulders, and stagger to stand on the sand at water's edge.

Jennie and Ben stood by helplessly. They watched as Gina's mother struggled back toward their blanket, carrying her daughter who finally, once her back was to the sea, had stopped shrieking and now, instead, was crying quietly into her mother's shoulder.

"Mental," said Felix, who had followed Gina's mother back down from the blankets.

"You don't know that!" Jennie replied quickly.

"Well, then, doctor, what do you think?" Felix teased. "I mean, it's not like we see people going bananas every day out here."

Mac Love, having run to the water with others, couldn't imagine a different explanation.

17

Gina huddled quietly in the back of Mrs. Johnson's van, her head leaning against a windowpane, her eyes closed. Her arms were wrapped around herself and her knees were drawn up onto the seat. She could hear what her mother was saying. She hardly cared.

"The whole thing was just so unexpected, Sally," she was explaining to Jennie's mother. "Something like that had never happened, an assault in broad daylight in a public swimming pool."

"The poor thing," Mrs. Johnson sympathized. "What a terrible memory to carry around."

"We've had counseling, both of us. And up until now Gina's been terrific and brave and full of common sense. I guess the noise and the water were just too much for her."

"It will take years, I imagine," Mrs. Johnson said, "to get past something like that. How awful."

"Oh, how we hope not," Gina's mother said quietly. "Kids are resilient, after all. And Gina knows that what happened wasn't set in motion by anything she said or did. It was something she had no control over. I suppose, when you think about it, moments like that are beyond anyone's control."

Gina imagined Mrs. Johnson shaking her head. "I think you should take the van and drive her home. You can come back for us later, when things are quieter."

"No, Sally, that would ruin everyone's day. We'll just—"

"Really, I insist," said Jennie's mother. "You can come back for us when life is calmer."

"Well, I really appreciate this, you know. Sometimes you just don't know what to expect or where to turn."

"Well, as you say, we can't always control what we'd like."

"I know, I know. And with my schedule, it's even worse. Sometimes I'll have to be at the hospital for days running. Sometimes at night, or all weekend. It's so hard to be on hand for every moment you need to be. I feel so guilty about that."

Stop feeling guilty, Gina said to herself. Please! Let's get out of here!

18

Gina's mother switched on the van's ignition, maneuvered a bit, and pulled away from the scene at oceanside.

Colors returned to recognizable range; sounds died to normalcy.

Within a few hundred yards Gina began to breathe more easily. She unwrapped herself and leaned up to speak to her mother.

"Was it really awful, what I did?" she asked, touching her mother's shoulder.

"Darling, I don't honestly think you had any choice. It's almost like what they call posttraumatic syndrome, where you suffer symptoms and memories for years after something terrible happens."

"I do feel better now," Gina said.

Her mother smiled in the rearview mirror. "You'll feel even better when we get home."

The drive wasn't a long one, from Hendry's Beach to their rented bungalow on La Plata Street. A few of their neighbors were out in the sunshine, working on their lawns or in their gardens. One man was washing his vintage Thunderbird in his driveway. No one seemed to notice or to care that Gina and her mother were home from the beach early.

"Come on, sweetheart. You're probably exhausted."

Gina stood outside the van, breathing deeply. She could smell the sea air where she stood, and knew that by walking a few hundred feet closer to the ocean, she would be able to see it.

"I think I'll just stay out and breathe awhile, you know?" she said.

"Want to walk to the park?"

The park overlooked the ocean. And the ocean . . . Gina sighed. "Sure."

At the end of the block, and across Cabrillo Boulevard, was a bright swatch of lovely green, with wind-shaped pines and yew trees. Gina and her mother walked slowly toward the overlook, down La Plata, a street filled with mismatched houses of different designs and hugely different values. The Mesa, the area in which Gina and her mother had found a place to live, was a changing neighborhood.

Traffic was light on the boulevard and they crossed easily. Both slipped off their shoes to feel the thick grass beneath their feet. They walked in unison toward a railing above the sea fifty or sixty feet below.

They stopped and leaned against it, their hands on the cool steel. Gina's mother put her hand over her daughter's and together, silently, they stared at the oil rigs out beyond Santa Barbara Harbor.

After a few minutes, Gina pulled her hand away and turned to embrace her mother. "Thank you," she said. "I feel a lot better now. Shouldn't you start back?"

"There's no rush, sweetheart."

Gina turned to look out over the water. She wondered what her mother would say if she told her what really frightened her. It wasn't the splashing at the beach, although that was what had set off her screams.

Instead, it was that one long, long moment when Gina, scrunched into the sand and screaming as water hit her, looked out into the face of the ocean and remembered. Back home, at the swimming pool, her only means of escape would have been to swim out into the deep water.

And at the beach, under attack again, the thought had returned to her with terrifying clarity. Here, too, escape lay in swimming out into the deep water, into the ocean. All she would have had to do was stand, run, and dive. No one would have caught her. No one.

19

Gina felt calm for most of the rest of that Saturday. Until she thought ahead to Monday. Going back to school.

She half expected with both dread and anticipation that Jennie might call her. The two weren't really best friends yet, but Jennie had been the first girl in her class to treat her warmly, and for this Gina was still grateful. It would have been nice to talk, about anything, even about what had happened at the beach.

Sunday's mist lifted well before Gina got out of bed. When she did, she dressed quickly—trying, as she had done for nearly the past two years, to ignore what she knew were the causes of all the trouble she'd experienced—and went into the kitchen where her mother sat at the table reading the Sunday *News-Press* and having coffee. "How did you sleep?" her mother asked.

"O.K.," Gina said, drinking from the glass of orange juice at her mother's place. She set the glass down with a definitive noise. "Mom, I can't go to school tomorrow," she announced flatly.

Her mother looked up and waited.

"Well, could you?"

"I don't know, honey. I know I wouldn't want to. On the other hand, since I would have to, sooner or later, I think maybe I'd grit my teeth and go just to get it over with."

"How do I get over these?" Gina wailed, indicating her breasts.

Her mother sighed, but not unkindly. "You grow into them. As you reach your full height, everything will be in proportion."

"But suppose you're wrong!"

"What do you mean?"

"Suppose they're always going to be huge!"

Gina's mother sipped her coffee thoughtfully. "Well," she said after a moment, "I suppose if and when the time came, when you had reached your full stature, and if you were still unhappy, something could be done."

"Why can't it be done now?" Gina asked, her voice breaking. "Now is when it's important!"

"Doctors don't like to do those operations too soon, sweetheart. No operation is easy, as I've told you before. Every time someone invades your body to do something to it, you run a hundred different kinds of risks."

"Well, no more than if I just hacked them off!"

"Gina! What a horrible idea!"

"You're a nurse. You could see that nothing bad happened, that there wasn't any infection."

"I don't think this is a very profitable conversation, honey. I know you're upset. And I understand how you feel. Believe me, if there were anything I could do that would make life easier for you, I would. But there really isn't. That's the awful part about being a parent. You can only protect in certain ways . . . and for such a short time."

"Well, I've got to do something!" Gina moaned. "I can't scream bloody murder every time I'm near water!"

"You won't have to, sweetheart. After all, it wasn't the

swimming pool that went crazy and attacked you. It was those boys."

"Oh, fine!" Gina scoffed. "I just scream every time an innocent eighth grader passes too close?"

Her mother smiled gently. "I imagine there are better solutions."

"That's what I was talking about, Mom! About school. About an operation. Those are better solutions."

"Right this minute they might seem to be, but not in the long run."

"Could I at least change schools?"

Her mother stood up, her coffee cup and saucer in hand. "You'd have to be bused who knows how far and how long. I thought you told me buses were for children."

"Well, I'd meet new people, make new friends."

Her mother carried her dishes to the sink. Then she turned and, leaning against it, asked quietly, "Gina, would you like to see another therapist, a new one, out here?"

"What for? He, or she, would just tell me what I already know. And I do know it. What I'm afraid of is that the boys at school don't."

20

"Do you want to come with us?" asked Ben Derby's father as he drank his coffee, having already showered, shaved, and dressed.

"I'd be the only kid there," Ben answered.

"So, you'd get along. You're very good with people, son."

Ben shook his head. "Besides, isn't Grandma coming over? It's Sunday. What about lunch?"

"I said I'd call her after discussing the brunch with you."

"But the brunch is for you, you and Valerie. It's all your friends, not mine. I'd be out of place. People would be too careful. Besides, they may not even want a kid around."

"They'd be pleased as punch to see you, I know."

"No," Ben said with finality. "Call Grandma. I'd rather see her."

"You're sure?"

Ben nodded.

Two hours later Ben's grandmother's car wheeled to a stop in the driveway outside. Ben slicked down his red hair as best he could and went to the front door.

"Are you making the Bloody Marys?" she called from the car.

Ben grinned.

"I don't know," said his grandmother a minute later, leaning out to kiss Ben's cheek lightly. "Living this high up, amid all the glitter. It's a long way from where I grew up."

"Me, too," Ben agreed, holding open the front door for her.

She paused and looked seriously at him. "So, darling boy, what do you think of it all?"

"What? The house?"

"You know exactly what I mean," said his grandmother, moving past him into the large vaulted family room and directly over to the wet bar. "I guess I'm on duty here," she added, pulling up two glasses and opening the small refrigerator below the counter. "You like yours spicy or dull?"

"Are you kidding?"

His grandmother shook her head. "I figure if the French can serve their children table wine from four or five up, we can certainly serve our kids a little something when they're thirteen. Just one won't do you any harm. And you can trust me. Your father will never know."

Ben grinned. "O.K. Dull, then. I get enough spicy stuff at the restaurant."

He watched as his grandmother snapped ice cubes from a tray and dropped them into the glasses. She bent down to bring up a bottle of vodka from which she poured, her own share twice what she put in Ben's glass. Then she added tomato juice, daintily sticking a finger in Ben's to stir it, and slid it across the bar toward him. For herself, she added Tabasco sauce and lime juice.

"Cheers!" she toasted, raising her glass finally, indicating Ben should join her in the ceremony.

"Cheers," he said obligingly.

"Do I have to do all the cooking, too?"

"No," he replied. "Valerie . . . she left a quiche in the kitchen. And she made a salad before they left."

"Let's check it out," suggested Mrs. Derby, picking up her glass and coming around from behind the wet bar.

Together she and Ben walked into a gleaming square kitchen, full of hanging copper pans and utensils, spotless counters, and a view over Santa Barbara that would make visitors gasp.

"Well, I give her credit," his grandmother said. "She's certainly trying."

"I know."

"But—?"

"So . . ." Ben prompted in return.

Mrs. Derby grinned. "I like your style, kid," she said.

"I like yours."

She took a sip from her drink. "We can't be too critical, I guess. We're not marrying her."

"I just thought Dad was, well . . . you know, like everything was organized in his life and all."

"And you were comfortable that way?"

"Sure. We have a good time together."

"You and I, Ben, we're both being selfish, you know."

Ben nodded glumly, trying his drink at last.

"Men like women. Most men, anyway. And your father certainly likes women."

"I know. We talked about it."

"You did?"

"Sure. Of course we did."

"So it's just this one, this Valerie, you're not crazy about?"

"Are you?" Ben turned the question around quickly.

"Not as much as I'd like. But it's none of my business. That's something you learn as you get old, Ben. There are just millions of things in this world over which you have no control."

"Well, she is pretty."

Mrs. Derby drained her Bloody Mary and started back toward the bar. "She's got the equipment, all right. I wonder how much of it is real."

Ben stood absolutely still, openmouthed.

21

"Gina? It's Jennie."

"Oh, hi!"

"I called, well, I just called to say hello and that, well, I know tomorrow is going to be—"

"Probably hairy."

Jennie laughed into her receiver.

"It's nice of you to call. I'm glad you did," Gina said after a moment.

"Well, my goodness, of course I would. I just wasn't sure how you were feeling yesterday."

"Shaky."

"From what your mom told mine, you've plenty of good reason."

"Yeah, but still—"

"Gina, for heaven's sakes! What happened to you was awful!"

Gina wasn't sure what to say. "It was only one time," she replied rather lamely.

"I don't see how anyone could have gone through that and stayed sane!"

Gina smiled at that. "Well, I feel fairly sane."

"Still and all, what happened was, well, unusual."

"I know."

"I'll meet you at the front doors of school tomorrow, O.K.?"

"Sure. But—"

"No buts about it. You need someone to cover for you, to protect you."

"Maybe I do. I don't know."

"We show a united front, in time people will forget all about it."

"You think?"

"I think. Besides, you're my friend. At a time like this you need people on your side, people who understand."

Gina was a little startled. First, she doubted Jennie really could understand what had happened and how it had affected her. Second, there was something in the way that Jennie spoke that made Gina wonder what exactly Mrs. Johnson had told her and maybe the others. She knew what her mother had told Mrs. Johnson. But what was it the others *heard*?

She went to bed that night as uncertain and as nervous as she had been the night before going to the beach.

22

School that Monday was an unreal experience.

Boys kept an almost suspicious distance.

Girls hovered, comforting and concerned. And dying to ask questions.

Gina saw it all.

And understood part of it.

23

MacNulty Love wasn't certain what to make of the scene at the beach on Saturday. It was fairly clear to him that he had witnessed something rare. Girls just didn't start screaming and shaking for no reason, as far as he knew.

It had been horrible to watch. He had been frozen, staring, hearing Gina's shrieks, and unable to move forward to do anything to help her. He didn't know what had set her off or what frightened her. It couldn't have been being splashed by a four-year-old. All you had to do about that was get up off the sand, scowl at the kid, and move.

Mac kept his ears open at school. He knew kids were talking, but often he caught only single words left hanging in midair after a discussion had ceased. "Weird." "Wired?"

To choose between those two possibilities was something Mac felt not up to doing. How could he? He had spoken maybe five words to her, especially if he didn't count the very first day of school when he had shyly asked if Gina would like a ride home with his mom. And at the beach he had been tongue-tied near her.

He thought Gina was beautiful. She was tall and filled out and always pleasant and, what made her most appealing to him, always a little off-balance, a little nervous, being new, anyway. He imagined her feelings were almost like his own. He knew everyone in the eighth grade, of course, because he had grown up with them. But because he was short, most people seemed somehow to miss him in a crowd, to accept his presence without comment in classes. Sometimes he would hang out with other guys, but he always felt—unless he was running—somehow younger than his peers, and he knew that wasn't true. He was actually older than Felix and Ben and even Eddie Phipps.

24

"I looked it up in *Webster's*," Eddie Phipps announced proudly at Felix's house late that afternoon. "*Assault* also means 'rape.' "

"Yeah, but it probably means other things, too," Ben said.

"I told you guys."

"Oh, Felix, come on! You couldn't have known!" Ben objected.

"A hunch," Felix said lazily, sprawled on the couch in his living room. "But you know I'm right. I called it. I told you. She's dying for it. Again."

"Only this time smooth and easy," Eddie said.

"Not from you, dickhead," Felix announced.

"Why not?" Eddie asked. "Who's better than me? I'm tall, I'm strong, I know what I'm doing."

"Says who?" Felix wondered. "Got references?"

"Come on, guys. This is dumb."

"Look, Benny banana, all I'm saying is that we have a ripe one here. Someone's got to pick the fruit."

Silence hung in the air thickly.

"Why not?" Eddie asked suddenly, the smile on his face mirroring the idea in his mind.

"Why not what?" asked Ben.

"Why not all three of us?" Eddie answered brightly.

"Are you kidding?" asked Ben, shocked.

"Not for a minute. I mean, this girl's *hot*. It'll take a lot to put out that fire. Sure, I could do it myself. But that would be selfish."

"You wish!" Felix laughed softly.

"What's wrong with the three of us doing it?" Eddie asked. "I mean, if she goes for it, what's wrong with that?"

"And how do you plan to get her permission?" Felix's tone was more sarcastic than enthusiastic.

"Yeah," Ben wanted to know.

Eddie nodded his head wisely, smiling still. "We warm her up. I don't mean physically. I mean, we get her to like us, to trust us. Then, when the moment comes, we jump her."

"Who goes first?" Felix challenged.

Eddie was firm. "I do, of course. It's my idea."

"I'm not taking any sloppy seconds," Felix objected quickly.

Eddie looked at him a moment. "Hell, I don't care. You can go first. I'm not squeamish."

Ben sat wide-eyed. In spite of what his inner voices told him, he was excited.

25

Alone, Felix lay lounging on the sofa in his living room, his eyes half closed, a smile on his face.

"Feeling pretty smug, are you?"

Felix's eyes snapped open. He did not turn his head.

"Didn't you guys know I was back there?" asked his sister, Raquel.

Felix shrugged.

"You're out of your head, creep," she said, almost in a whisper.

Raquel took another step into the room. She was the younger of Felix's two older sisters, nearly eighteen. She was as thin as Felix, but her face was rounder, more inviting. "I hope to God Mother didn't hear you," she warned.

"She's still at work."

"You're wrong there, too, wise guy," Raquel informed him. "She came home early with a cold. She's in her bedroom."

Felix shifted on the couch and half sat up, looking at his sister expectantly.

"Look, I know what hormones are," she told him. "And I know what guys your age think about, all the time. There's nothing wrong about that, Felix. But if you get mixed up in the kind of thing I heard, you're dust."

"So you say."

"Jesus! Don't you get it, Felix?"

"Get what, exactly?"

"I assume you know what 'rape' means."

"It's not rape if she agrees."

"Forget it," Raquel said quickly. "According to what I heard, it's rape, pure and simple, no matter how smooth you guys think you are. No kid her age is going to take all three of you on."

"You don't know that."

"I'll tell you one thing. If I knew who you guys were targeting, I'd get to her and let her know."

"Yeah, but you don't know."

"Maybe not, but I know something else, something worse."

"Such as?"

"Think about this, Felix. Think about your last name. Moldanado. What does that kind of name mean to people?"

"Who cares?"

"You will, wise guy. And so will the papers. And so will her parents. Not to mention your own mother. And trust me, it's a long name for Eddie Phipps to hide behind. You're getting older. How come you're just as stupid as you've always been?"

26

Having felt like an object of curiosity the day before, Gina felt slightly better at school on Tuesday.

As before, Jennie hovered protectively in the classes they had together, in the cafeteria, in the halls. Every time Gina sensed a boy looking at her, examining her, Jennie, too, sensed the moment and diverted her attention.

But not all boys were as hard and suspicious as the day before. Ben, with Jennie at his side, seemed more or less normal. Once, during first lunch, Gina caught him looking at her with puzzlement. But as far as she was concerned, confusion was a lot better than hunger.

Ben's friend Felix seemed always on the outer rim of a circle, looking in. His eyes were the ones Gina feared most. He seemed more adult than other kids she knew, more knowing. And she didn't think she would like to hear everything he knew or was thinking about.

The big surprise of that day was Eddie Phipps. Before, Gina had accepted Jennie's opinion of him. "He's just a spoiled bully," Jennie had said the week before. "He sort of sticks out. He'll probably be sent away to school, anyway, which is too bad because he's not terrible-looking. And he has a great bod. But what girl wants to tie herself to someone who's going to disappear just when life begins to get interesting?"

Well, Gina might, she decided. He seemed concerned about her. His eyes were full of sympathy and interest. He didn't speak to her often, apart from saying "Hi" in the halls or smiling sometimes at her across the one class they shared. But Gina thought he was sort of cute, and so she smiled back at him. After all, winter was coming, and she had been told to expect gray skies and lots of rain. Also a lot of hanging around a nearby mall, and movies. As much as she needed a friend like Jennie, she wanted to have a boy nearby to hang with, too.

27

In the cafeteria on Wednesday, Eva Pajerski put her tray down next to Gina's and Jennie's. "Hi," she said, sliding into a chair beside Gina.

Gina smiled. She hardly knew this girl.

Eva began unloading her tray. She spoke very quietly as she did so. "I hear you had some trouble back east."

Jennie glanced at Gina and leaned in closer.

Gina wasn't certain what to say. She looked at Eva, a roundish girl with a complexion that was perfectly creamy, gray eyes, and sun-streaked hair. Finally she nodded. "A little," she admitted. After all, her mother had told Jennie's mother, had had to give some kind of explanation for Saturday. No doubt Mrs. Johnson had returned to the kids on the beach and done her best to explain to them what she had been told. And from there—well, kids talk. There wasn't any point in trying to keep the boys at the pool a secret anymore.

Eva opened her wrapped taco. "Maybe I could help," she said, still in a low tone of voice.

"Help?" Gina asked, feeling dumb.

Eva nodded as she bit into her food. "We have something in common," she said around it.

"We do?" Gina asked. "What?"

Eva reached for her Coke. "Are you busy after school?"

"No, I guess not," Gina said, ignoring the nudge she got from Jennie.

"Let's talk then," Eva suggested, turning and smiling warmly at Gina.

Still at sea, Gina nodded after a moment. She would take Jennie with her.

28

The three girls stood together under a clump of trees a hundred yards from the school's front doors. Eva had said nothing about Jennie's presence. It didn't seem to trouble her in any way. She focused all her attention instead on Gina.

"The same thing happened to me," Eva said evenly.

"What do you mean? What happened?" asked Gina.

"I was raped, too."

"Raped!" escaped from Jennie's open mouth.

Eva did not turn in Jennie's direction. "Last year, in seventh grade."

Gina listened, stunned.

"By someone you knew?" Jennie asked.

Eva nodded at Gina. "A friend of my brother's," she said.

"But Gina wasn't raped," Jennie objected quickly.

Eva looked steadily at Gina, waiting for her to confirm or deny what Jennie had just said.

Suddenly Gina's thoughts were multiplying in a fascinating but awful way. "Is that what people are saying?" she asked. "That I was raped?"

Eva nodded, her eyes steady. "No one knows about me," she admitted after a moment.

"Did it happen more than once?" Jennie asked then.

"No," Eva said, turning finally to face Jennie, seeming a little angry. "Would you let someone that close to you again? Would you let someone like that even be in the same room alone with you after that?"

Jennie was silenced.

"Well?" Eva asked Gina again.

"I wasn't raped," Gina said, "and I'm so sorry about what happened to you, Eva. Really. How terrible."

"Yeah, well, it was bound to happen sometime or other, wasn't it? Boys need that kind of thing."

"But not rape," Gina objected.

"I know," Eva agreed. "We always dream about it differently, with blue lights and music. But it's life."

"But didn't you tell your mother?" Jennie asked. "Didn't you report it to—to someone?"

Eva smiled sorrowfully and shook her head. "The damage was done. What's the point?"

"Well, to keep him from doing that to someone else, at least!" Jennie answered decisively.

"Jesus!"

"What, Gina?" asked Jennie, alarmed.

"People are actually saying this!" Gina replied in despair. "I mean, I'm in a swimming pool, for God's sake. A public swimming pool. If people think that's what happened, what must they think of me?"

29

"It's easy!" Eddie Phipps explained that same afternoon at Felix's house.

"Sure," Felix drawled.

"I've got it all planned."

Ben leaned forward in an easy chair. He didn't feel he had anything to say, but he was excited to listen. Maybe.

"Look, smart-ass," Eddie said, "I've already got her smiling at me."

"Oh God," Felix snorted. "That's certainly a sign of hot pants." He shifted on the couch, grateful that his sister Raquel wasn't around to hear any of this. And that his mother, despite her cold, was back at work. "All right, Einstein, prove it."

"Well, the first thing we need is a car."

"What for?" asked Ben, surprised.

"To get over to her house, for God's sakes!" Eddie sounded exasperated.

"That's where you plan this thing happening?" Felix asked, amazed. "In her own house?"

"Where else?" Eddie demanded.

"In the car," Felix said simply.

Eddie shook his head. "No. That's too much trouble. I mean, can you see each of us climbing over the seat into the back, one after the other, to take turns? Number one, she'd scream bloody murder. Number two, we don't want—at least I don't want—everybody listening and watching while I'm at it."

"So what is the plan?" Ben asked.

"O.K. I get one of my parents' cars and pick you guys u—"

"Hold it," Felix said, raising his hand. "How do you plan to get away with that? Can you even drive?"

"Sure I can. And it's easy to get a car. I just take my basketball and walk out of the house through the garage. We've got electric door openers. What I do, see, is push the button, to make anyone who's around think the door is going up all the way. But then I push the button again, stopping it. I slip out and play around, bounce the ball a little, a few minutes. I wait awhile, to see if anyone's interested. Then I stop and go back to the garage. I push the button again, which sounds like the door is coming down again. What's really happening is that the door is finally up all the way. Then I get in, start the motor, and let the car glide down the hill to the street. From there on I'm golden!"

Felix shook his head doubtfully. But he waited. So did Ben.

"So, then I come to pick up you guys."

"Where does she live?" Ben asked.

"I'm not sure yet, but by the weekend I'll know."

"So," Felix said, jumping ahead, "you plan to arrive at her house, not knowing whether she's even alone, and you expect her to open the door and invite three hungry studs in to do what, exactly? Study geography?"

"That isn't what I had in mind," Eddie said, almost angry now at Felix's resistance.

"What is?" asked Ben.

"Well, first of all, one of us has to break down her

defenses. Get her to warm up a little. Show her he's a good guy. Gain her trust."

"So over her shoulder she looks and sees two more guys ready to jump her?" Felix wanted to know.

Eddie shook his head. "You don't get it. One of us—maybe we choose straws—goes in first and does it. Then, when he's finished, he leaves and the next guy goes in."

"You passing out condoms in a relay?" asked Felix.

Eddie grinned and stood up from his chair. "Nope. I'm doing that right now. Courtesy of my old man's top drawer."

He handed out small square plastic-wrapped packets.

"What happens if her mother's there?" Ben asked then.

Eddie sighed. "Then we wait. Nothing's lost. We've made a new friend. We've shown we're not strong-arm guys. We're all pals. And we wait until some day, or night, when she is alone. The better we get to know her, the better our chances are."

"And you figure, if that happens, you can grab a car again without being caught?" Felix wondered.

"Why not?" Eddie sounded confident. He leaned back into his chair and grinned again. "Look, my parents are in cyberspace. They don't know what's going on at ground level, either of them. They're upstairs noodling around and making money or something. They won't even know I'm gone." He paused dramatically. "So you see, it can be done. No sweat."

"No sweat," Felix echoed. "Jeez, you're crazier than Benny banana here. Sweat is what this is all about!"

30

Ben pedaled slowly and with great effort back up into the Riviera section of Santa Barbara.

He couldn't stop thinking about the plan, and about Gina.

And he couldn't stop imagining having sex for the first time.

Deliberately, he pushed aside the troubling thoughts: that Gina was being taken advantage of; that somehow this whole scheme was not honorable.

If what Felix and Eddie suspected was true, if she had had sex already, then maybe she really would allow what they planned to happen. Maybe she would figure that since the first time hadn't been so great, she might as well try again and see if it got any better. Ben had read often enough in magazines and books about how people, when they had their first experiences, didn't have a good time. That knowing what to do and how to do it in order to give pleasure to both partners took time and consideration.

He heard the word *consideration* in his mind and batted it out of his consciousness.

His father's car was in the driveway when Ben arrived at home, puffing and out of breath. He put his bicycle in the garage, thinking how unusual it was that his dad would come back from the restaurant at this hour. He wondered what was up.

"Hi, kiddo!" said his father when Ben appeared in the

kitchen. Mr. Derby was standing at the window that overlooked the city below, a cocktail in his hand. "Got a treat in
store for you tonight."

"What?" Ben said, suddenly suspicious.

"Valerie's taking us both out to dinner!"

Oh. "She is?"

His father nodded enthusiastically. "She says that she's
had enough Tex-Mex to last her a lifetime. That we boys
had better learn to appreciate a little French food from time
to time. So she's coming by to take us over to Montecito."

Ben didn't say anything right away. What he thought
was that he'd rather try new foods at Felix's house, where he
knew Irene was a terrific cook and where she usually introduced Felix and his friends to culinary surprises slowly, step
by step. "Can I ask you something?"

"Sure, son. What?"

"When you had sex for the first time, how old
were you?"

"Whew!" his father exclaimed, taking a large swallow
from his glass. "That sure comes out of left field." He
paused. "Let me think."

Ben waited patiently.

31

"That's what they think!" Gina nearly wailed as she and her mother sat in the kitchen. She had hardly touched her dinner.

"Oh, honey, I'm sure not."

"Look, a girl I hardly know came up to me today to sympathize. She really had been raped, by a friend of her brother's. She was going to give me advice!"

Gina's mother sat silently for a moment. "Remember that old game Telephone?"

"What are you talking about?"

"Well, that's what I imagine happened here. When I spoke to Jennie's mother about what happened—you heard me—my guess is that she went back to the beach and tried to explain to the kids there what had happened. I mean, they all had seen something they couldn't explain. Chances are the story somehow changed, got altered in people's minds. *Assault* became *rape*."

"Oh, terrific!" Gina sighed. "What am I supposed to do? Go around and tell everyone that what they think didn't happen? Isn't that like what Dad used to say? How could a man stand up and announce to the world he didn't beat his wife? The very words convinced everyone he did."

Gina's mother smiled sadly. "You have a point, I admit."

"You know," Gina said then, her voice taking on an edge of desperation, "back there, in that swimming pool, all I wanted to do was swim out into the deeper water. If I could have done that, I could have escaped." She paused, not meaning to be dramatic but realizing that what she was going to say would upset her mother. "Well, at the beach, that's what I thought, too. Sitting there on the sand, I could get up and get away by leaping into the ocean and swimming out and out and out. I could get away. If only I were brave enough."

Her mother's mouth opened but no sound came out. Finally: "Oh, Gina. No. No, darling."

"It's true." Gina persisted, feeling stronger now that she had shared her horrible vision.

"Darling, nothing is that bad. Truly."

"I don't know, Mom. I think maybe this is."

Gina's mother pushed back her chair. She put her arms around her daughter's shoulders and hugged her tightly as she spoke. "Sweetheart," she said, "listen to me."

Gina sat enfolded in her mother's embrace.

"I am very, very proud of you. I'm grateful that we can talk this way, that you told me about how you felt at the beach."

Gina nodded.

Her mother's grasp became even tighter. "Promise me something."

"What?"

"That if ever, ever you have feelings like that again, you'll come to me. Promise you won't do anything until you do. Promise!"

32

"I tried to get hold of you last night," Jennie said urgently when she met Ben outside school the next morning. "Where were you?"

Ben shrugged. "Out with my dad and Valerie. She took us to dinner. Her treat."

Jennie's eyebrows went up slightly. "She doesn't sound like such a bimbo to me."

Ben wasn't sure what to say. "I guess she's not bad. She's trying."

"It can't be easy, Ben," Jennie said. "I mean, she's moving into a pretty tight little unit. And she's not going to be your mother."

Ben nodded. "That's what she said to me last night. Strange. She said she wouldn't be, and wouldn't try to be. Just that she hoped we'd come to like each other and to trust each other."

"I think that's very adult."

Ben laughed slightly. "You do?"

"I certainly do. But that's not—Listen, Ben, I think there's a huge storm coming."

"From where? I didn't hear anything on the weather."

"I'm speaking metaphorically, Ben Derby. Stop patronizing me!"

Ben grinned. "Oh," he teased.

"I am serious. We've got a situation here."

"We do?"

"We don't. Gina does!"

With a start, Ben wondered for the first time how Jennie would react when she heard he and Felix and Eddie Phipps had done the deed. Purposely he'd never considered this before. He looked away, into the crowds of students arriving for classes.

"Pay attention," Jennie said smartly. "Listen, Ben, the word's out that Gina got raped back east."

"Um-hmm." Best not to be too up front.

"You know?"

"Yeah."

"Well, it's not true!"

"Says who?"

"Gina, that's who. And I believe her." Jennie sighed. "But that kind of rumor can really ruin you."

"I don't see how if it's not true," Ben half lied.

"Oh, for God's sakes, Ben Derby, think!" Jennie urged. "Just think a minute. People say you're loose and begin to get ideas. Your reputation's up in smoke."

"So how'd you find all this out?" Ben asked, beginning in the back of his mind to worry: if what Jennie was saying was true, then he'd better get to Eddie and Felix.

"Well," Jennie said slowly, thinking how much she should say, "a girl, someone from our own class, came up to Gina yesterday to offer sympathy. She really was raped. And she thought she could—"

"Who?"

"Never mind. You wouldn't pick her out in a thousand years."

"How do you know she was telling the truth?"

"Ben, people don't lie about things like this. Think."

Ben was thinking.

And he was watching, as Gina and Eddie strolled toward school, walking close together, talking quietly. Eddie had a smile on his face and seemed to be explaining something to Gina, who listened as she walked, giving him quick, sidelong glances.

33

"So we've got to get hold of Eddie and tell him, call him off!" Ben said almost under his breath when he met Felix at lunch.

"How can you be sure what Jennie says is true?"

"I just am. Felix, we'd be ruining the girl. We can't do this."

"But what if she wants it?"

"You don't know that!"

"Hey, I admit I was wrong once, back in sixth-grade math. But not since then, Benny boy."

"Felix, you're not listening," Ben insisted. "This is serious."

"So is getting our rocks off for the first time."

"With a crazy girl?"

Felix shrugged with half-closed eyes. "Why not? Who's going to believe her when they've already seen her go bananas?"

Ben stood up from the cafeteria table. "Jesus!" he said angrily. "I begin to actually feel a little sorry for her."

"Don't," Felix advised. "Trust me. This girl has been hot since she got here."

"In your dreams!"

Felix nodded contentedly. "Exactly, Benny. In my dreams."

"But what about reality?"

"Hey, there's real and there's real. No sweat. What we've

got here is damaged goods. She's been thrown on a dump. All we're doing is picking her up. Salvaging her."

"I don't believe you," Ben said.

Felix started to laugh. "No sweat, and 'No Fear'!"

Ben turned and walked away in a hurry. For the first time in his life he didn't like Felix very much.

34

"We are definitely making progress," Eddie reported after school as the three boys hung over various pieces of furniture at Felix Moldanado's house.

Ben watched Felix, waiting for him to share with Eddie what Ben had told him earlier.

"Yeah, I saw," Felix said eagerly. "She really seems to like you."

"Why shouldn't she?" Eddie boasted. "I mean, I'm the Best in the West."

Felix laughed. "God knows at what!"

"Look, wise guy, I've got this thing bagged. She likes me. She smiles. She talks. I mean, when I walk in that front door, I'm going to be welcome!"

"What happens when you walk out?" Ben asked quietly.

"Hey!" Eddie replied. "Then you guys walk in!"

"Sounds easy to me," Felix agreed.

"You're not going to say anything, are you?" Ben asked his best friend.

"About what?" Felix played dumb.

"About what I told you at lunch."

"What?" Eddie wanted to know. "What are you talking about?"

"Jennie told me that Gina wasn't raped." Ben's tone was cool.

"She what?" Eddie was surprised. "How does she know?"

"Because Gina told her," Ben answered. "Pure and simple, what happened was that she was attacked in a swimming pool and, well, groped and . . . you know."

"It's the 'you know' we're interested in here, Benny boy," Felix said. "Ever since this kid arrived, she's been throwing it around."

"She hasn't," Ben shot back. "She's just, well, endowed."

"Listen," Eddie said slowly, thinking as he spoke, "listen. No girl her age is going to say anything else. I mean, it's like child abuse. What kid is going to scream about being hit on? Think of the trouble that causes. Lawsuits. Trials. Family crises. Embarrassment."

"Yeah, I agree," Felix said quickly. "The minute she says she was raped, guys like us are ready to jump all over her."

"Well, we shouldn't," Ben announced. "It's not fair. We're taking advantage of her."

"Not at all, Ben," Eddie said, standing tall and leaning against the back of an armchair. "We're bringing her happiness. It's what I said before, sometimes you need care and tenderness to get over a bad scene."

"And that's what we're providing?" Ben asked, almost astonished. "Not just jumping in order to be the first on the block to have an experience?"

"Well, kid, that's what Felix and I are going to do. What about you? Are you in or out?"

35

"Is Jennie there, please?"

"Oh, hi, Ben. Sure, wait a sec. I'll get her."

The moment was a long one for Ben.

"Hi," Jennie said happily into her receiver. "What's up?"

Ben had a quick dirty thought but suppressed it. "It's about what you told me today."

"What?"

"That Gina wasn't . . . you know."

"Raped?"

"Yeah."

"Well?"

"Well," Ben said, uncertain what exactly to say and how far to go.

"Yes?"

Even at a distance Ben reddened. "Well, maybe she should sort of be careful, you know?"

"No. What are you saying?"

"Well, it's just that I heard some guys . . ." Ben paused, but he felt relieved that he had found a solution.

"Yes?"

"Some guys, you know, thinking about what people say about her."

There was a moment's silence on Jennie's end.

"What do you mean, 'thinking'? You mean 'talking.' "

"I guess."

"And what else?" Jennie's voice had grown hard and suspicious.

"Well, I guess thinking that since that was supposed to have happened once, how—how bad could it be if—"

"You're kidding!"

"No. It's just what I heard." Ben paused. "Will you sort of warn her?"

"This is sick!"

"I'm not arguing. I'm only reporting."

"Who are these idiots?"

"Just guys, in school. You know."

"I don't know, and if you do, you tell me, Ben, right now!"

Ben didn't feel he could do that.

36

"I may not be able to pick you up, sweetheart," Gina's mother said as she slowed her car in front of the school.

"How come?"

"Well, I'm warming up, I think, to the late shift. That is, my bosses are warming up to that idea. So today I work until eight. Tomorrow the same."

"Just because you're new?" Gina asked.

Her mother shook her head. "No, darling, it's part of the job. It's what caring for people means. You can't always be free when you want to."

Gina nodded. "Still, what about your personal life?"

"I've got one, haven't I?" her mother laughed. "But when you're on call, people who need you don't stop to think about that. And it's right they shouldn't. They have to depend on us, on our being there when we're needed."

Gina opened her car door. "Well," she said, "I can always walk home. Or maybe get a ride."

"There are buses, too, sweetheart. Don't forget. Just get home safely."

Gina had barely turned away when Jennie Johnson was at her side. "Gina! Thank goodness! We have to talk!"

37

After hearing Jennie's news, Gina walked the halls Friday scrutinizing faces. She looked into eyes, saw who looked back and, more important, she thought, who didn't. By the end of the day she had counted more than twenty boys who could be suspects. In what, she wasn't exactly sure. Just twenty boys she had to be careful about.

She got through her classes, barely paying attention. During lunch with Jennie, Gina had had to try, gently, to shut Jennie up. If what she had told Gina was in the air, was around a corner, Gina felt it better not to focus on it. That's what she thought.

But she couldn't get the rumor or its meaning out of her mind.

When the bells rang at the end of the day, Gina stepped through the doors into the sunshine outside and, without turning her head, started down a walkway.

"Hi."

Mac Love was at her elbow. She hadn't even seen him.

"Oh, hi, Mac."

"TGIF, eh?" he said shyly. His voice sounded more nervous than happy.

"I guess."

"Want a ride home? My mom's car's just over there," Mac said, pointing.

"What?" Gina began walking again. "No, it's all right. Really. But thanks."

"Gina?"

"Hmm?"

"I was thinking. Maybe tomorrow you'd, well, sort of like to go to the movies with me."

Gina stopped instantly and turned to look at Mac Love. A cold look, she hoped.

"I mean, if you'd like to," he stammered.

Gina stood amazed that she hadn't considered Mac Love all day.

"There are three or four good movies on State Street," Mac said. "We could take a bus, or maybe I could get my mom to drive us."

The alarms that had been clanging in Gina's mind began to quiet. Not with his mother around, she thought. Not on a public bus. Not in a movie theater, although he might try to grab.

"Well," she said slowly, still weighing and measuring, "maybe. You could call me."

Mac's smile was wide. "O.K.," he said. "That's what I'll do. I'll look in the paper tomorrow and then give you a call. O.K.?"

Gina's smile was genuine. "Sure. Give me a call."

38

He was king of the world. Master of the universe. Stronger and faster and smarter than anyone in the galaxy. Women fell to their knees. They begged him to kiss them. They lay at his feet, looking up at him adoringly, hoping to be chosen.

He stood with his legs apart, his arms folded over his huge chest. He looked down at them all, thinking, selecting. Imagining.

Then he saw her. He saw her first at a distance, standing as though waiting for him to approach. She was unafraid. She had as much experience, as much knowledge and know-how as he had. She was offering to match his heat. She stood amid low clouds, a kind of fog that eddied in and around her full figure. She was sure of herself.

He waited a moment, glancing down at the others who cried out to him, whose hands still tore at his clothes. Then he looked at her again, standing alone, unblushing, confident, inviting.

He started to walk through the hordes of women on the ground. He knew without looking that eyes filled as he passed, that sighs were launched in his direction, that disappointment was the fog he parted as he strode manfully toward her, the other, the chosen one.

They stood face-to-face. For a moment neither moved. Then, as though having agreed without speaking, he and she raised hands to the other's shoulders to begin the undressing.

Before his hands had even touched her, they could feel her glow.

✦ ✦ ✦

He was sprawling on a lounge chair, a cushioned piece of outdoor furniture. There was a drink at his side, on a small white table. Overhead, attached to the sky, was a white wooden fan, whirling and spinning, blowing just the faintest cool air down onto his body. He closed his eyes and smiled to himself.

And opened them again at her touch. She stood beside him, swaying to the music of guitars that played on a track somewhere. Maybe there was a band, just out of sight.

In her hand was a tray of tapas and snacks. And a pitcher of the same drink in his glass. The pitcher was clear and he could see fruit slices in the dark liquid. He nodded at her coolly, not moving a muscle other than those around his mouth.

She understood. She put the tray down on the table beside him and then took a step backward, silently waiting for his examination.

He looked at her, containing the excitement he felt at her presence. He twirled a little finger in a circle then, and she turned slowly before him. He admired her figure, her breasts, the flow of her thin cotton dress.

Suddenly he could hear a distant rumble of thunder. The air above was clear and blue, but he felt certain that was what he had heard. He waited a moment, and then inwardly shrugged.

He looked again at her, grinning.

She stepped out of her sandals.

Then she moved closer to him, smiling invitingly. She bent down over him, her hair falling to cover his face.

Like a serpent suddenly aroused, his arm came up quickly and, roughly, with his hand he brought her face down to his. He kissed her, gently at first and then more firmly.

She yielded without a word.

✦ ✦ ✦

They were running, hand in hand, up a hill, away from people who called to them from below.

At the top of a rise they stopped, breathless. They looked at each other and laughed, happy to be away, to be free.

He put an arm over her shoulder. Together they looked back down at the small knot of people, people still calling to them.

He thought some of the crowd looked familiar. He frowned. He didn't want them to be.

He turned to look at her. She stared back into his eyes, trusting, waiting.

Although he could hear, even from a great distance, some of the people below shouting at him, he put his arms around her and brought her body toward his. It was time. This was supposed to happen.

✦ ✦ ✦

He was racing. He was tall and fast and determined. He could hear the cheers of a crowd somewhere nearby, but

*when he took a quick glance to one side, he saw nothing
but open countryside.*

*The tape shimmered ahead of him, unattached but taut,
waiting to be split. He leaned forward and broke it with
his chest.*

*And there she was, her arms around him, hugging him,
proud of him.*

*Suddenly both of them were surrounded by family and
friends. He recognized his father, his mother, his older
brothers, and, since he was older now, their wives.*

*Everyone was smiling, happy. He took her hand in his
and swung it a little. She gripped it firmly, squeezing
encouragingly. They eased their way out of the
congratulatory crowd and began, side by side, to climb a
small hill, from the top of which they would look down and
wave. He could feel her hand in his, and he felt as though
their hands were bonded somehow, meant to be together
for all time.*

*At the top of the rise, they turned together. But instead
of looking down at his friends and family, they locked eyes.
He understood both his message to her and hers to him. He
took a step closer. . . .*

A weight suddenly landed on his bed, rousing him. He
leaned up on an elbow, knowing he would see Opal, his
family's wire-haired terrier. He smiled sleepily and stretched
out a hand to scratch her head.

39

Eddie Phipps woke early. He was smiling to himself as he rose into consciousness. Today was the day.

He thought about calling Felix immediately, but then he looked at his bedside clock-radio and decided against it.

Across the room lay his set of weights, barbells, and dumbbells on the floor, a towel over the bench.

Well, he would exercise then. There was a goal. There was something to work for.

Besides, he wanted Gina to get a real stud, not have to put up with some skinny street kid from New York.

He got out of bed quickly and went into the bathroom. When he emerged, he tore off his T-shirt and laid the towel on the bench carefully. He sat at one end of it and, still grinning, reached out for a pair of forty pounders.

By the time he got to wherever his parents were planning on sending him, he'd be ready to take on anybody.

And he would have joined the statistical ranks of teens who had had a sexual experience in high school. The papers and television were full of those reports. Hah! In his case, he would have made it happen in eighth grade!

He imagined telling his new friends at boarding school about everything. He could imagine their faces, their big eyes, their opened mouths, eager for every detail.

40

Ben woke and, realizing what lay ahead for the day, brought up his bedcovers and shrouded himself in them.

He thought about Felix and Eddie and himself arriving at Gina's door.

Maybe her mother would be home.

God, he hoped so!

He shook his head at his own thoughts. Here he was, a bright kid, ready for sex. And he felt like running away from it as far as he could.

Not from sex so much, he thought, uncovering his head to stare at the ceiling, as from the circumstance of the event.

He thought of what his father had told him the other day about his first time. What he remembered most clearly was the difference between what Eddie and Felix and he planned and what his father had said to him.

Because even though it had happened to his father and a girl who turned out not to be Ben's mother, his father had thought he was in love. And so had the girl. They had made love because they both wanted to, because they felt something terrifically strong for each other. And they had been happy.

No matter how hard he tried, no matter what Eddie said about giving Gina happier memories than those she had already, Ben couldn't honestly make a comparison between the two stories—one real, one so far imaginary—that made him feel comfortable.

And what would Jennie do if she found out?

She would, Ben knew. Even if Gina herself said nothing about the three of them, Jennie was smart.

He closed his eyes again. Maybe he could stay in bed all day, hiding out. He could phone Felix and say he was sick.

Except that Felix would know he wasn't. And so would Eddie when he heard.

Worse than anything, Ben would have to listen to Eddie and Felix boast and crow and relate what happened and what he had missed and how terrific it was.

Angry at himself, Ben threw back his covers and stood up. He put on a robe and left his room, walking into the sunlight that streamed through the house from tall windows and skylights.

"Well, kiddo, you're an early riser."

His father was in his bathrobe, too, sitting on a bench in the breakfast nook, sipping coffee and leafing through the Saturday morning *News-Press*.

"Yeah, well, I was thinking, Dad," Ben started, not really knowing what was going to come out of his mouth.

"And?"

"Well, I have to admit I may have been a little tough on Valerie. I mean, the other night she was really nice."

Mr. Derby put down his coffee mug and leaned against the upholstered back of the bench. "I'm happy to hear that, son," he said. "She really is fond of you, you know. She wants to make a success with you."

Ben nodded. "I know, I know," he admitted. "So I thought, well, I mean, does she ride a bike?"

"Gee, Ben, I've never asked her."

"What I was thinking was we could all three ride out to the beach and have a picnic. I'd make the sandwiches. You and she wouldn't have to do anything. I'd make iced tea and everything. We could spend some time together, you know? Get to know each other better."

"Valerie may have plans for the day, son."

"Why not call her and see?" Ben suggested eagerly, beginning to like his own idea and feeling instantly lighter of heart once he'd heard it.

41

"O.K., stud. I should be there around three."

"You know where she lives?" Felix asked.

"Yeah. The Mesa."

"Your folks home?"

"My mother's in Los Angeles. Dad's upstairs working. He won't even break for lunch, and then he'll take a nap. Says you shouldn't fight the urge to sleep when you need it. He doesn't. This is a piece of cake, believe me."

"So what if he wakes up?"

"I told you, Felix. This is a two-step operation. Step one, open the garage door partway. Wait awhile. Step two, open the door all the way, making it sound like you're closing it. Then, with a little luck, I'm out of here and at your house in twenty minutes."

"What time?"

"Like I said, around three. Three-fifteen."

"O.K."

"Hey, buddy, by nightfall, we'll all be Men. Ben'll be with you, right?"

"Right. I'll get him here in time."

"Good, because I don't know where his house is, and since we're going to be all fired up, I don't want to dissipate our energies driving around town."

"You mean 'waste'?" Felix couldn't help teasing.

"Damn. Yeah, that's what I mean."

42

Irene Moldanado stood in the doorway to their living room. "Ten minutes, Felix. Don't tell me you forgot, and please, put on a different shirt. Your aunt likes to see you dressed up a little."

Felix looked around at his mother and nodded. He liked looking at her. She was comfortable and easy on the eyes: a little round, always neatly dressed herself, capable. She gave her children confidence, and she was also able to discipline them without anger. What had to be done had to be done. There wasn't any use in arguing.

"The whole family's going to be there?" Felix asked, pulling himself off the couch, up from his usual slouch.

His mother smiled. "We've had reunions before, Felix. Of course everyone who can be will be there."

"It's for dinner, right?"

"Yes. Why, do you have a late date?"

Felix reddened. "No, ma'am. Just wondered."

His mother shook her head a little. "Sometimes you make me wonder, Felix." She turned away and went back toward her bedroom at the rear of the house.

Eddie was going to go ape-shit, Felix knew. The thought didn't make him sad. The only problem was, he hadn't been able to get Ben on the telephone to alert him. If Ben showed up, even if he guessed the right time, what then? He'd be really pissed.

Felix shrugged and started toward his bedroom. Raquel

was right. If anything went wrong, if Gina struggled or fought or was hurt, if she talked, it was the Moldanado name that would stand out in the *News-Press*. Phipps and Derby might be mentioned, but people would see the Moldanado and nod. Sure. Of course.

The world running the way it usually did, chances are Phipps wouldn't be in the paper at all. Eddie's old man would buy silence. As for Ben, his father was well known and liked. Maybe the *News-Press* wouldn't name his family, either. It would really hurt his mother.

As he changed clothes, Felix wondered if he should say something to Raquel, not quite "Thank you" but something.

He decided against it.

But when he had finished dressing, he walked into the kitchen to see her at the sink, washing the dishes from lunch. Silently, Felix walked to her side and picked up a dish towel.

43

Eddie stood motionless at the door in *his* kitchen. He listened. He waited. Nothing.

He twisted the door handle silently and slipped into the comparative darkness of the garage. His father's Mercedes, being black, hardly glimmered.

Eddie walked quietly to where the interior buttons were for the garage door opener. He held his breath and pushed. With a low rumble the door behind his father's car began to rise.

When the door was halfway up and there was enough room below it to slip out onto the driveway, Eddie pushed the button again. The door's movement halted. Eddie scooped up his basketball and slipped out into the sunshine of the driveway.

Again he stood without breathing, listening. Then, as though just fooling around, he let the ball drop and began to dribble it a bit. He turned from about twenty feet away and launched the ball toward the rim of the basket hanging above the garage. The ball didn't make a sound as it passed through the net.

Eddie grinned broadly. "All right!" he muttered to himself. That was surely a sign of something, something good. And he knew what that something was.

44

It was just after three o'clock. Everything had happened as Eddie said it would. He had started his father's car and eased it out of the garage, turned slowly, and headed downhill. When he hit the street, he turned right and started down to Coast Village Road which, after he took another right, would eventually lead him to the freeway and then up to Felix's house.

Eddie was so excited by driving the car and by imagining what would happen when he got to the Mesa that he purposely focused diligently on what he was doing. The last thing he needed now was to be picked up for speeding. He stayed at exactly the speed limit, not the extra five miles an hour almost everyone else drove.

He eased the Mercedes to the curb in front of Felix's house. He wondered if he should honk. He decided not. Someone might ask who was picking Felix up and for what. Someone might even ask who was doing the driving.

He sat, idling the car for a moment. "Hey, guys," he said under his breath, "let's get this show on the road. Come on!"

He waited another few moments before, impatiently, he turned off the motor and got out of the car. He walked up the path toward Felix's house, expecting Felix and Ben to come out quickly when they saw him.

He stood on the front porch. By leaning over a little, he could look into Felix's living room. He saw no one. A little angry, Eddie knocked on the door.

Then he knocked more loudly and stood back, waiting.

45

"Jesus Christ!" Eddie said to himself out loud as he drove away from Felix's house. What had gone wrong? Had Felix said anything to his family? And where in hell was Ben?

Well, it didn't matter. He hadn't gone through all this to be put off. He was ready. She was ready.

Eddie imagined himself as a locomotive tearing along the track. Get out of the way, world. Here I come. Smashup time.

He sat up straight in the driver's seat and looked at his hands on the wheel. He tightened his grip and watched the muscles in his forearm bulge.

Destiny.

He grinned to himself when he thought that word.

Fate, he amended.

46

The day was warm and slightly breezy, perfect for flying kites or strolling a beach or bicycling.

Gina felt safer indoors.

She lay curled on a couch in her living room, watching a rerun of an old Julia Child cooking show. Gina wasn't fond of cooking, but she loved the way Julia's voice swooped and scooped, and the way she so neatly swept crumbs from her workstation onto the floor beneath her feet. Gina had often wondered who was down there, off camera, behind the table, waiting with a broom and dustpan. It amused her to think of her own mother trying to do this.

She hadn't forgotten about Mac Love and the movies. But he hadn't called, and she really wasn't all that disappointed. Maybe he would just appear.

47

At first Gina didn't hear the faint knocking on her front door. The volume on the television, and Julia's dramatic whoops, didn't allow one to concentrate on much else. When the knocking grew louder, however, Gina got off the couch and went into the front hall. Cautiously she looked through a side window to see who it was.

She stepped back quickly, feeling herself blush. She would never have expected him.

She ran her fingers through her hair and smoothed down her sweatshirt before opening the door.

Eddie Phipps stood on the threshold, a gigantic smile planted on his face. He held his hands together behind his back, posing as an old-fashioned suitor. "Hi," he said. "I hoped you'd be home."

"Hi," Gina said shyly, smiling at him.

"Want to go for a ride?" Eddie asked. He stepped sideways and pointed. "I've got my dad's car. We could tool around for a while. Maybe get some ice cream or something."

"Oh," Gina said, Eddie's age not registering, "I'd love to, but I can't."

"How come?" Eddie asked, his smile diminishing.

Gina shrugged. "Well, I'm sort of waiting for a call."

Eddie looked at Gina for a long moment without speaking.

"But there's ice cream here," she said, " if you want to come in."

"Well, if you're sure it's all right."

"Sure," Gina said. "Come on in."

He paused on the threshold.

In the living room Eddie said, "This is pretty neat. Nice colors."

Gina nodded. "We like it. We were lucky to find it. The kitchen's through here."

She led him to it.

"This is a great kitchen, you know?" he said. "It's homey. Ours is sterile and huge. It doesn't look like anyone ever cooked or made a mess in it."

"It's cozy," Gina agreed. "Now," she said, walking to the refrigerator and opening the freezer compartment, "what kind would you like?"

Eddie followed her across the small room. Gina looked over her shoulder at him. He seemed very close to her and very tall. "What have you got?" he asked, staring into her eyes.

Gina turned away and put an arm into the freezer, lifting first one container and then another. "Walnut, coffee, French vanilla, orange sherbet."

"French vanilla," Eddie elected, putting a hand out to rest on the refrigerator, his arm to one side of Gina's shoulder. "Anything French is pretty sexy, right?"

She tensed, then laughed a little and pulled out the carton. When she turned around, Eddie's other arm was stretched against the door. They were face-to-face.

They stood a moment, looking at each other.

"Here," Eddie said finally, reaching for the carton, "I'll take that."

He removed the container from Gina's hands. He put it slowly on top of the refrigerator and then dropped his hand and arm into their earlier position, encircling Gina. Without looking at her, he also moved his body closer to hers. She could feel him against her.

"Eddie—"

"What?" he said, his arms sliding down to grasp both her hands in his.

"Uh . . . the ice cream . . . will melt."

"Uh-huh," he said, pulling her hands apart and positioning them behind her back. They were body to body now. Alarmed, Gina wondered what he was looking at, for his eyes were focused somewhere past her ear.

Without another word, Eddie pushed his body hard into hers. His hands gripped her own, trapped them really, behind her back. His face ducked down into the spot between her neck and shoulder, and he was kissing her skin there, roughly.

Gina looked up at the ceiling, panicking. "Eddie!" she said. "Stop. Stop it!"

"Come on, babe," he whispered into her neck. "Come on, baby."

Gina began to struggle. But Eddie's body had her pinned against the refrigerator door. She couldn't free her hands, no matter how hard she wriggled and pulled.

Then suddenly Eddie let her hands go and brought both of his up to her chest.

"Stop it! Stop!" Gina cried.

But he didn't.

His hands moved over her breasts and down to her waist, her hips, and back up again. "Oh, baby," he whispered, "I've been dreaming."

Gina was frozen for a moment, until Eddie's mouth again began nibbling on her neck. She looked up at the ceiling once, as though for guidance, and then she leaned forward quickly into him and bit his neck below the ear.

"Ow!" he said quickly, moving back a few inches.

Suddenly freed from all of Eddie's weight, Gina jabbed her knee into him, hard.

"Ohh!" Eddie gasped, backing away, his arms instantly protecting his crotch. "Jesus!"

Gina broke away and ran out through the living room. She opened the front door and continued onto the small front lawn. She was struggling for breath, frantic to figure out how to escape.

Eddie appeared at the front door, still doubled over. She could see the anger on his face, the surprise.

"Get in your father's car and get out of here, or I'll start screaming," Gina said with every ounce of courage she could summon.

Eddie stood on the front step for a moment, looking at her. Glowering, he started to walk toward her. Gina backed away, closer to the curb, her mouth open, ready to scream. One false move. "One false move," she warned him.

Eddie kept walking toward her and then, miraculously, past her. He walked around the front of his father's car and pulled open the driver's door. "Whore!" he cried bitterly.

"What's one more scene? I'm a hell of a lot better than what you've had already!"

He slid into the car seat as Gina stood speechless on her lawn.

She didn't move until the Mercedes had slowed at the corner and turned left, back toward downtown Santa Barbara.

She was shaking. She wanted to collapse there on the grass but felt some neighbor might see and come over. Instead, she turned and slowly made her way back to her own front door.

Once inside she began to sob.

48

Gina hunched in a high-backed armchair, shaking and crying. After a few moments she tried to stop shaking, gripping both arms of the chair and planting her feet firmly on the carpet, sitting rocklike, staring straight ahead at nothing.

Suddenly she felt warm. And angry. Not just at Eddie Phipps but at herself. She had been warned by Jennie. She had let down her guard. She had been flattered by Eddie's attention.

She should have known better.

Bitterly, she smiled, thinking of how her alarm signals had rung when poor Mac Love had asked whether she'd like to go to the movies.

Without being aware of what she was doing, or why, she stood quickly and began pacing the small living room, throwing her arms about, her eyes blurring again. She scolded herself. She should have known. This kind of thing was always going to happen. In eighth grade, in ninth. There was so little she could do, so little any girl could do.

Then, as though in a dream, she opened her front door. She crossed the patch of grass that was her front lawn and headed toward Upper Cabrillo Boulevard, to the lovely park that overlooked the sea.

Recklessly she danced between cars and made her way across the busy thoroughfare. On the other side she slipped off her shoes to feel the grass between her toes. She approached the steel fence that guarded the overlook.

Gina leaned against it and looked out for a long time. Finally she looked down. But the sea wasn't what she wanted it to be. It was quiet. There were no huge rollers crashing onto the rocks so far below, no surf roaring. All her emotions were just that, hers alone. Nature wasn't in tune with the growing despair she felt.

The sea below ebbed and flowed, breaking gently and gradually, easing up toward land and then slipping away again almost silently.

If only she could do the same.

She stared down at the water. There was a definite pull to the tide. It might be fun to ride it out again with a slight swoosh. And then just to let go, allowing the sea to do with her what it would.

If she had to look forward to Eddie's kind of assault all her life, was life the great good ride people always said? Not if they were carrying the same baggage she was.

She tilted more closely to the fence and continued to stare down at the sand and rocks. She argued silently with herself. How could she change? What was it that lured boys to see her as they obviously did? She nudged away the simple answer. It wasn't just because of her figure. It had to be something else. But what? And how could she learn what it was? And if she did, could she change? Could she change anything and still be herself?

"Hi."

Gina turned very slowly to look over her shoulder. It was Mac. She tried to smile at him, but she couldn't. She turned again toward the sea.

49

"I took a bus over," Mac said. "My mom couldn't drive us, after all."

Gina nodded without looking at him.

"Are you all right?" Mac asked. "Are you mad I didn't call?"

She shook her head. "No," she said. "No to both."

"Want to walk down to the pier?" Mac offered.

"No."

"Well, then, maybe we could—" Mac stopped in mid-sentence.

Gina had spun around toward him, and he couldn't decipher what her expression meant. He was startled at first by the intensity in her eyes. And he was amazed when she took a step toward him and threw her arms about his neck and began to cry into his shirt.

Still not understanding, Mac felt very, very tall.

50

Eddie Phipps eased his father's car into its usual spot in the garage and then, pushing the garage door button, congratulated himself on his stealth and success.

Success at something, anyway.

He opened the door to the walkway that led to the kitchen and tiptoed in. At the kitchen table sat his father, nursing a cup of coffee. "Nice of you to show up," said Mr. Phipps.

"Hi, Dad," Eddie said, thinking he could bluff his way out of anything.

"The car O.K.?"

Eddie blushed. "Sure, I guess. Why shouldn't it be?"

"Because my fourteen-year-old son has been out joyriding in it. If you weren't my son, I'd have called the police."

"Hey, Dad, I just wanted to try it out, you know. Nothing heavy. Nothing serious."

His father nodded rather sadly. "Well, here's something that is. You're grounded. Period. Until I feel I can trust you again. You'll be driven to and from school every day. No visiting other kids when school is over. No movies. No TV, and no time on the computer. No parties. No sports."

"But Dad, all I did was—"

His father rose quickly from the table and held out a hand. Eddie put the keys to the Mercedes into it.

"Now disappear," said his father angrily. "I don't want to see you or hear you. Your mother will get you something to eat. Just stay out of my way."

Mr. Phipps left the room quickly, his face flushed and angry but determined. Eddie knew that look and, while he wasn't afraid of it, it gave him little hope of easing around his father for a while. The question was, for how long?

He shrugged. After all, he hadn't been punched or creamed or hit or anything like that. Of course his parents never had done such things, but still, under pressure, they might, Eddie supposed. There was always a first time.

He climbed up to his own room and closed its door behind him.

Shit! What a perfect day! Betrayed by his friends, kneed by that slut, and now grounded by a father who wouldn't easily forget or forgive.

He walked into his bathroom and snapped on the light. He stood for a moment at the sink, looking at his reflection in the mirror above it.

He brought a hand up to his neck and pulled down the edge of his T-shirt.

There it was.

He stared at the mark for a long time.

Then he smiled at his own face.

Perfect!

He knew exactly what to do on Monday.

51

Sunday

Eddie hoped, when he came downstairs, showered and brushed and in clean clothes, to make a good impression. And that his father's anger and dismay from the day before would have abated. They hadn't.

Mr. Phipps, on seeing his only son appear at the threshold to the dining room where he was about to have breakfast, stood and, pausing a moment in the kitchen door to speak to his wife, said, "I'll have mine in the library, dear, if it's not too much trouble." He did not even glance at his son as he left the dining room.

Eddie waited a moment and then went toward the kitchen himself, smiling as widely as he could. "I'll do that," he offered, without having the slightest idea of what in fact his mother was doing.

She did not turn from the stove. Rather, with a wave of her hand, she indicated the kitchen table where a place had been set.

Eddie shrugged. The silent treatment.

Life could be worse.

He sat at the table and waited. At least, he thought to himself, Mom is still serving.

✦ ✦ ✦

Felix awoke slowly and lay in his bed, grinning. He'd had a great time at his family reunion. It amused him to remember that every time he hadn't wanted to go to a party somewhere and had been made to go, the day, or night, had turned out to be terrific.

If he hadn't gone, he wouldn't have met Serena.

He closed his eyes to picture her: compact and well distributed, a happy smile that could pull back if she got nervous, but—toward him, anyway—real warmth. He tried to think of how to see her again, but she lived almost forty miles away. It wouldn't be easy.

If he hadn't gone to the reunion, what would have happened?

He snickered to think. He knew Eddie Phipps. He knew Eddie was a big talker.

There wasn't a doubt in his mind that Eddie had chickened out. First of all, he couldn't just steal his dad's car. God, what was that idiot thinking about? Grab a car and you could be slammed into jail for who knew how long? Felix had already decided, before the reunion had come to his aid, that he wasn't even going to get into the car, assuming Eddie had actually stolen it.

Second, Eddie Phipps was no more smooth than he was. Both of them could dream, and imagine, and talk big. But when experience counted, neither one of them had any to offer.

If what he had all along thought about Gina was true, she had the edge there. She'd probably whomp Eddie the minute he made a move.

Screw Phipps, Felix decided.

He closed his eyes and thought again about Serena.

Forty miles wasn't so far.

✦ ✦ ✦

Ben woke, hopped out of bed, and slipped into jeans and a T-shirt, then grabbed Baines's leash to take the dog out for his early-morning relief.

The morning mist was rising, and although there were streaks of blue above it, Ben also saw heavier, darker clouds moving in from the north.

Well, let it rain, he thought. Saturday had been great, and he couldn't wait to tell his grandmother about Valerie and the picnic and cycling and the good talk he'd had with his dad when they returned home.

"Valerie was happy you thought of her, Ben," his father had said. "And so am I. That's an adult approach to what might have been a difficult problem. You've made it easier for us all, son. Thanks."

Ben had flushed, to be complimented so openly.

"Now," his father had continued, "if we can only get your grandmother and Eileen to open up the same way, why, hey, maybe we'll have a happy family for the next forty years. What do you think?"

What Ben thought as he replayed this conversation in his head was that, for a whole day, he'd forgotten all about Felix and Eddie and Gina and the plan.

He wondered whether Felix and Eddie had carried it off.

Felix would tell him. He'd probably get a call right after Felix got back from mass.

Well, Ben decided, there wasn't anything to do. He felt good about not joining the other two. He had made the right decision. Felix might crow a bit, and Eddie certainly would. That was O.K. He'd get around to "it" in his own time.

✦ ✦ ✦

Mac Love and his family went to church and then out to lunch.

52

Gina's Sunday was as confusing as her Saturday had been.

When Mac had come to the park, and after the relief she had felt nearly gave her away, Gina had pulled back. Mac was blameless. The fact that he was a boy didn't make him guilty and brutal as Eddie was.

Pulling herself together there at the sea's edge, Gina had stepped back and away from Mac.

She realized as she looked at Mac's expression—one of puzzlement but also of pride—that she would have been safe if only he had arrived earlier, with or without his mother in the family car. But that was what might have been. Now Gina knew she had to deal with what was real.

Instantly she understood that her only hope lay in silence. Her own and, oh God, please! Eddie Phipps's.

She had, after all, walked down to the pier with Mac. Together they had spent perhaps an hour before he decided to go home. Gina had helped with his decision, saying there were things she had to do before her mother got back from work. Mac was still at sea over her behavior, she knew, but he was easily and sweetly guided.

Once more alone, Gina sat again without moving in a chair in her living room. She was debating and countering her own arguments at the same time. As twilight fell, she still hadn't been able to answer her own most important question: should she tell her mother what had happened?

She and her mother were two women alone. Together

they had weathered her father's desertion and then, later, the divorce. Together they had supported each other and been cheerful and optimistic about the future.

Gina's mother had been comforting and calm and warm after the incident at the pool. Without her, Gina couldn't imagine what she might have done or down which mean streets she might have chosen to walk.

Together they had been counseled about that afternoon in the water. Gina's mother felt guilty she hadn't been able to save her daughter from the attack. And Gina herself, no matter how well intended the therapist's questions, couldn't let go of the feeling that it was something she had done, or said, or been that had drawn the boys to her in the water.

By the time Gina's mother returned from work this Saturday, Gina had made a light supper for herself and taken refuge in her bed.

She couldn't ask her mother to move again, to pull away from another town because something weird had happened to her. Her mother would never have a chance at a life of her own if, every time someone hit on Gina, the two of them had to flee.

Yet Gina understood that by not confiding in her mother as she had done for so many years, she was, in a way, staking out independent, and unknown, territory. Would it be fair later, if something happened, to lean again on her mother's shoulder when she had been silent about this?

"I'm just whacked," her mother sighed after knocking on Gina's door. She pushed it open. "How are you?"

Gina looked up from her nest of pillows and cush-
ions and books and tried to appear lighthearted and normal. "Fine."

"Well, my knees have slipped to my ankles and I'm
bushed!" Her mother grinned. "I've just enough energy to
fall into bed. See you tomorrow, sweetheart."

"O.K., Mom. Night."

She had made her choice.

So on Sunday, Gina chatted and laughed and smiled.
While what she did felt right to her, Gina also felt badly
about deceiving her mother. Ultimately, she thought, she
needed this day to grow up.

Not a lot of fun.

53

On Monday, school wasn't as bad as Gina had feared. It seemed that Eddie Phipps had said nothing to his pals.

When she had seen him in one class, or later, in the halls, neither he nor she had looked in the other's eyes. In fact, Eddie seemed embarrassed and had turned away each time.

By last period Gina was feeling relief. If no one knew, and if Eddie wasn't going to blab, then maybe, just maybe, she could get on with her life, no matter what. Idly, as she took her chair in history class at two-thirty, she imagined telling Jennie about what had happened on Saturday.

But not now. Maybe next year, when kids had scattered and moved on to other schools. Until then all Gina could do was hold her breath and hope, and with every moment that was easier to do.

54

Eddie Phipps was a few seconds late for his last class, English.

So were Ben and Felix, and two more of their friends, who followed him into the classroom.

He had the mark to prove it, the hickey. Not only had he had sex, he'd told them, but he'd gotten away with stealing his father's car!

Of course, being the gentleman he was, he kept the details of initiation sketchy. "Guys," he said smoothly, "no one talks about that. That would be really gross."

But being pressed, he did allow that Gina had been a wildcat. Just look at the mark on his neck. And while he'd like to tell them more, he couldn't; his mother, he said, was picking him up right after school.

55

Ben didn't know what to think. He believed Eddie. Why not? Eddie had the evidence.

Maybe Felix and Eddie had been right all along. Once you got a taste of something, you hungered for it more and more.

There was no one else in his class Ben could think of who might have had anything like Eddie's experience.

He thought a minute, in his chair before class began, about Jennie Johnson. If Gina really was a girl like that, who could blame someone for giving her what she wanted? It wouldn't have anything to do with Jennie and him. After all, boys were supposed to have experiences like this. It made them better husbands and lovers.

He shook his head, knowing he would never get this line past Jennie. And he really didn't want to.

He liked Jennie. He had not liked himself for dodging the details of what he knew they'd planned.

He would try to make up for that moment of dishonesty. Jennie would never know why, but he would be nicer, more considerate.

Maybe they could have dinner at his dad's place later.

56

Tuesday morning Gina dressed for school, not really daring to hope that the day would be a good one. As she selected, once again, something fairly neutral and bulky to wear, she felt she was walking along a very thin ledge. At any moment she could lose her balance and fall to the street below.

That was exactly how she felt when her mother dropped her off at school that day, for the first person Gina saw was Jennie, pacing the steps near the entryway, clearly waiting for her.

The pit in her stomach opened instantly.

Gina tried to gather herself, to imagine what terrible news Jennie had. And she could.

But before she had to face her friend, she saw something else that made her cold all over and shaky.

A black Mercedes had pulled to the curb, and from it stepped Eddie Phipps. Worse, the minute his feet hit the sidewalk, he was surrounded by other boys. Eddie grinned and swaggered, clearly pleased to be the center of attention. He stood a moment without moving, basking in the admiration of his peers, apparently listening to their questions and congratulations. Then, not seeing Gina watching nearby, he drew himself up and started toward the front doors of school, followed by his troop of pals.

Just then Jennie's hand reached Gina's arm.

"You should have told me!" Jennie exclaimed. "You should have told me, and then the cops, and then the school and his parents and —"

Gina began to perspire. She felt weak. She held her books more tightly to her chest. Someone knew. Some *one?*

"How?" was all Gina could think to say.

"Well, because we're friends, first of all. And second, you can't let the creep get away with it."

Gina stared at Jennie a moment, uncertain how much or what exactly to say. "I meant, how did you find out?"

"Ben told me last night," Jennie replied quickly.

Oh God!

Gina stood a moment stunned, unable to move. What was she supposed to do now? "But nothing happened," she said finally. It sounded, even to her, weak.

"What do you mean, nothing happened?" Jennie asked. "Everybody in school knows."

Gina began to get angry. "What do they know?" she wondered sarcastically. "What could they possibly know?"

"Oh, Gina, I don't mean—I guess, what I mean to say is that they couldn't know, of course, what it was like or how you feel. But they know it happened."

"But that's what I want to know," Gina persisted. "What do they think happened?"

Jennie blushed. "Well, that—that you and Eddie . . ."

"Yes?" Gina waited, feeling increasingly angry, yet strangely patient.

"Did it." Jennie's voice was a whisper.

Gina nodded. Eddie wasn't bragging about how he had tried and been repelled. He was boasting that he had gotten through to her, had gotten away with it.

Jennie's grip on Gina's arm tightened. "He has a hickey, Gina."

"What he's got is a bite mark and very sore balls."

Jennie's eyes opened ever wider.

"We didn't do it, Jennie," Gina explained calmly. She felt as though everything she said and thought were coming to her from some distant place.

"You didn't?"

Gina shook her head. "He tried, but I fought him off. I kicked him in the crotch and ran. And that's all there was to it."

"But you let him into your house."

"My mistake," Gina admitted. "I thought he liked me."

Jennie shook her head in doubt. "I don't know," she began. "I mean, how can—I don't know how I could stop people talking."

"Neither do I," Gina said. "But I'll have to think of something."

57

Gina's mind whirled and eddied like the sea not so very far away. Actually being in a class was bearable. She couldn't see people behind her. She couldn't hear what might be said about her. But walking through hallways was another matter.

The bravery she'd managed to show Jennie had disappeared soon after she walked into the school. The coldness in her gut had returned, and the all-too-familiar shaking. She still carried with her the chill terror of the pool.

She tried to walk among her classmates with her head up and her eyes clear. But it was difficult. She felt herself lapse back into her slumped posture, cradling her books across her chest protectively, her eyes down.

She decided she would be able to make it through the morning, but the idea of going into a cafeteria, surrounded by curious and even mean classmates, was something she couldn't bear. She would go home. She would go home and wait for her mother.

Knowing that what she was doing was one part cowardice and one part intelligence, Gina slipped out of school when the bell for first lunch clanged, and walked slowly away.

She let herself into the house and stood a moment in the hallway, not really knowing what to do next. She wasn't going to cry. She promised herself that.

What she wanted to do was to call her mother at the hospital. She wanted to tell her about Eddie and his lies, how the kids in school believed them. She wanted to talk about what had really happened Saturday afternoon.

She put down her books and went back outside to the street.

Her mother would be enraged. Her mother would feel guilty, again. Her mother would want to sue or horsewhip Eddie or—Gina smiled to herself. She wouldn't argue about that.

She stood at the curb, a solitary figure in bright sunlight. She lifted her head suddenly. She could hear a breathing in the distance.

The sea.

Her telephone rang.

She wondered who was trying their number during the daytime when no one was supposed to be at home.

School? Her mother, already notified that Gina was missing? Jennie, with the latest horror story?

She stood listening.

After a few moments the ringing stopped, and in the freshened silence, Gina heard the ocean again.

She was drawn to it.

When Gina thought about the future, what she saw were the shadowed figures of other boys, older, in high school, trying to do the same thing to her that Eddie had. Where was the end to that sort of existence, always having to fight and defend until one day you were just too tired to do either?

What would she have done on Saturday if Mac hadn't come?

She wondered what he must be thinking, listening to Eddie's lies. Mac had nothing else to believe. She hadn't confided in him when she could have.

She crossed Cabrillo Boulevard toward the park.

Mac was a romantic, she decided, different from other kids in school and yet, apart from this single trait, not really. He was, they all were, kids who didn't know much of anything about life. Malls and movies and the beach. Clothes and music and computers.

Nothing real.

58

He couldn't have asked for a better day. As he came through the front doors of the school, Eddie looked down toward the street and there was his mother waiting, in the car, idling, the window on the passenger side down.

He gave her a cool, low-key wave and, knowing some of his troop was still following, started down the steps.

No kidding, he thought. He couldn't have planned it better. Of course she wouldn't talk. Wouldn't dare say anything. And now here he was, cock of the walk, ready for the world, armed, experienced, capable. He didn't even consider the falsehoods in this list. No one else knew them, and as long as that was true, he wouldn't ever have to think about them. If he was going to be sent away to school in the East, this reputation was something he could carry with him, build on.

The really big surprise had been how she had left school at lunchtime.

Well, he didn't blame her. What could she do or say that would make a difference? Nothing. Certainly not up against the physical evidence he carried—he slipped his hand below the collar of his shirt to caress the hickey—and there wasn't any physical evidence of her innocence that she would be brave enough to produce.

He smiled at his own thoughts. If she really was innocent, something he never for one minute believed, anyway.

He reached the sidewalk and turned, beaming at his

tiny crowd of friends. "Later, guys," he said, grinning and winking at them all. He pulled open the passenger door and stood there a moment before getting in. They knew he was a hero. He knew he was. Let them gawk for one more minute. He tensed the muscles in his arms and in his lats and stuck out his chest.

And then he was blindsided. Something came at him at sixty miles an hour, hitting him in the gut, pushing him back against the car door, whipping his neck over the top of it. The wind left him and he crumpled to the pavement between the curb and the car, landing hard on his knees and scraping his hands.

He was dumbly aware, as he started to look up, that the crowd around him had melted away. Instead of many shoes and jeans, he saw only one pair.

He raised his head further. All he could think was "No kidding!" when the fist caught him under his chin and he was up on his knees, falling back again into the car door.

59

Mac Love held his ground. He could have hit and run, and run fast. No one would ever have caught him. But that wasn't what he wanted.

He looked down at Eddie Phipps even as he heard Eddie's mother scream and open her car door to run around to help her son.

Mac stood still, waiting. When Mrs. Phipps knelt by Eddie's side, he relaxed finally, knowing his job was complete.

He cleared his throat and tried to bring down the register of his voice. "He's a scumbag," Mac said evenly.

"But what on earth, I mean, why did you—how could you—" Mrs. Phipps looked up imploringly at Mac, her arm around Eddie's shoulders.

"He's a creep, ma'am," Mac said. "I'm sorry you have to know. But you should."

"I'll get you," Eddie growled from the pavement.

"No, you won't!" Eddie's mother nearly screamed. Then, calming almost at once, she said to Mac, "We'll get to the bottom of this, young man."

"I hope you do," Mac replied. "But I wouldn't expect too much truth from your son."

"You'll have a lot to answer for," Mrs. Phipps warned.

Mac nodded. "My name's MacNulty Love. I'm around."

And then he turned and made a path between the few boys who still stood, amazed, nearby.

60

Ben swung off his bicycle and threw it against the side of Felix's house. He neither rang the doorbell nor knocked. He found Felix in his usual position on the couch. "You've been hiding all day," he accused.

"No, I haven't," Felix replied. "There just wasn't a chance to talk."

"Sure, sure. Not in the halls, not at lunch."

Felix closed his eyes slowly.

"You could have phoned over the weekend."

"Why?" Felix wanted to know. "Maybe you'd be mad I backed out."

"What do you think about all this?" Ben asked, throwing himself into a chair, genuinely curious. "I mean, what about that Eddie Phipps! Can you believe that?"

"You mean about his getting lucky?"

"That, and the hickey, and making it, and who knows what else?"

Felix shrugged and squinched around on the couch.

"Are you jealous?" Ben asked.

"Are you?"

"I don't know. I really don't."

"So how come you didn't call me?" Felix demanded suddenly.

" 'Cause I felt a little like a wimp," Ben replied honestly.

"You know what I thought?"

"What?"

"That Eddie needed us. That without a gang around to see what he was doing, he wouldn't go through with it."

"But he did."

"Yeah."

"So, what about Love?" Ben asked. "What was that all about?"

Felix shrugged easily. "Who knows? Maybe he hates Eddie Phipps. Maybe he loves Gina."

"You really think so?"

"Anything is possible. What's interesting, Benny old boy, is that no one rushed to help poor Eddie. If his mother hadn't been right there, Mac would have punched him silly."

"Well, he's not the easiest guy to get along with," Ben reasoned.

"Still and all, he's the champ. Isn't he?"

"Yeah, I guess," Ben admitted.

"He got there first."

Ben nodded silently and looked out Felix's front window at the street. "Maybe I better get going," he said.

"You can stay for dinner if you want. Mom's not home yet, but maybe she'll bring back something good."

"No," Ben replied, "but thanks." There was a sour taste in his mouth that could only be cleansed by leaving.

"You talk to Jennie?"

Ben was surprised. "Well, yeah, after school."

"You're lucky," Felix said. "I mean, at least she's in the same town."

"What are you talking about?"

Felix zipped his lip.

61

"My goodness! What is it, Jennie? Come in."

Gina's mother held open her front door, looking out at the curb where Sally Johnson sat in her car, its motor still running. The two women waved at each other. Mrs. Johnson asked in mime whether she should come in as well, but Gina's mother shook her head no. She left the girls alone in the living room and went out to chat.

"I'm sorry about knocking so loud," Jennie said breathlessly to Gina, "but I just had to see you. You disappeared and I—"

Gina smiled a little and put out a hand, indicating Jennie could come off high speed.

Jennie looked around the small living room impatiently. She wasn't seeing details or furniture. "Are you all right? Did you hear about Mac Love?"

"What?" Gina asked. "What about him?"

"He attacked Eddie after school, right in front of everybody. Right in front of Eddie's mother!"

"Why?"

"No one knows. I was hoping maybe you had told him what you told me."

"I didn't see him this morning," Gina said. "I haven't talked to him."

"Well, really, he beat the bejesus out of Eddie Phipps. He was like a whirlwind. Fast and tough and then totally still. I couldn't hear what was said, between him and Eddie, or between Mac and Eddie's mother, but you can guess what's coming next."

"I can?"

"Sure." Jennie went on, still breathless, frowning with concern. "There'll be a big confab at school. Eddie and his family versus Mac and his. And the principal and teachers will all get involved. One or the other or both will probably be suspended."

"But why? Not why about the fight, but why would Mac do what he did?"

Jennie stared at her friend a moment, waiting. When Gina didn't speak, Jennie rushed on. "Because he believes Eddie!"

Gina backed away from this revelation and sat down. She held her head a moment in silence.

"What are you thinking?" asked Jennie, kneeling.

"I don't know," Gina murmured. "Honest to God, I don't know. If you're right, then I've got Mac in a situation that's really awful. He could be kicked out."

Jennie shrugged. "But it was great he did what he did."

Gina laughed mournfully. "I suppose."

"We can go to the principal and tell him what's behind all this."

"No, we can't. You don't get it, Jennie. The last thing in the world I want is for everybody to know what happened, here or back east. The reason Eddie came on is because he heard rumors and believed them. I mean, if it's happened once, what's the big deal about a second time? That's not what I want people to know, or think."

"Well, then what?" asked Jennie, a little exasperated. "You've got to do something. Otherwise, this whole thing will—"

"I know what it will do," Gina said quickly. "It will follow me wherever I go. Every day people will look and point and whisper."

"Not if we talk to the principal."

"I can't. Don't you see? All that would do is make me more noticeable. I just want to shrink away and disappear."

They heard a car door slam outside and then the sound of a horn.

"I've got to go," Jennie said. "Are you coming to school tomorrow?"

Gina shrugged. "I don't know. One thing. I sure won't unless you swear here and now, on Ben Derby's blood, that everything we've ever talked about is sacred. I mean it, Jennie. On Ben's blood."

Jennie scowled. "That's so medieval."

"Swear."

"Come on! I haven't even told my mother!"

"Swear!"

62

"Mom! I am O.K.!" Eddie had told her firmly as she maneuvered the Mercedes away from the school.

"Don't be insane, Edward," said his mother. "You're bleeding."

"I'm fine, really. I'll recover."

"Whatever made that boy do that?"

Eddie shrugged. The less information he gave her, the better. He was already grounded. If his dad found out what he had tried to do after taking the car, he'd probably be shut up in the basement, put on bread and water.

"Do you and he have a rivalry of some kind?" his mother asked. "Did you have an argument?"

Eddie smirked a little. "About what? That kid, in a fair fight, would have been wiped off the face of the earth. He just had surprise on his side."

"Well, I for one am going to get to bottom of this. Tomorrow we'll go to the principal and find out what punishment he intends to dole out."

"No, we won't," Eddie said quickly. "Look, Mom, kids fight all the time. It doesn't mean anything."

"But I want to know why he attacked you, Edward. He must have had some reason, illogical though it may be."

Eddie sat silently a moment. He thought he knew why Mac Love had come at him.

But people believed his story about Saturday. People were in awe of him; they admired him. And why not? He'd got his hands on the best pair of hooters in school. That he hadn't gone all the way was a trivial detail he dismissed. That really didn't matter. He bore the evidence. As far as the guys knew, he had been to the mountaintop. He was a star.

He would never admit to his parents what had happened, what his intent was, or its outcome. A few days' suspension would only make his story legend. When he came back, he would be king of the world, just like in his dream. Girls would lie down for him everywhere he put a foot. By the time he got to whatever school his parents had in mind, the legend would have grown. He would write his own ticket in that place: captain of the football team, class president.

Looking out his window as the car climbed back to the safety of Montecito, Eddie smiled to himself. Not telling the truth, not telling much of anything about all this, was his ticket to success and fame.

The world worked in mysterious ways.

Cool.

63

"But she's got to do something!" Jennie warned prophetically.

At his end of the telephone Ben doubted that anything Gina did would really make her feel better. "What?" he asked sarcastically. "Go to a doctor and prove that nothing happened?"

"She could!"

"Then what? Hold up the report in plain view, telling everyone she's still a virgin?"

"Better than having everyone think you're easy, a target. You don't get it, Ben. She's been a target most of her life. With her body, she just sends out some kind of silent signal that says, Here I am, come get me."

"You think she really doesn't know this?" Ben was incredulous.

"God, you boys are all alike!" Jennie was exasperated and angry.

"Look," Ben said, ignoring the accusation, "people believe Eddie. Gina'd be going up against a guy who's a local hero. She's new. Who's going to believe her?"

"I am!" Jennie said quickly. "And you, too, I would hope."

Ben was silent a moment.

"Benjamin Derby, speak to me, right this minute!"

Ben waited another second. "Suppose she goes to the principal, or her family does. Suppose Eddie gets suspended or kicked out. Listen, Jennie, that's just more heavy baggage to carry around. She'd be the girl who ratted, who got Eddie sent away. What happened today wouldn't even have anything to do with Mac Love. It would be Gina's fault. No one would ever trust her again or even want to be her friend."

"I would. I believe her, entirely. Why do you guys insist on believing Eddie Phipps's lies?"

"Who said we do?"

"It's obvious, Ben. You're protecting Eddie because you want to. What if Eddie came to school and announced he slept with me? Would you believe that, too?"

"No," Ben replied quickly, "because you I know."

"Would you ever try what Eddie did?" Jennie asked then, veering away from the earlier subject of make-believe.

Ben blushed. He stammered what he knew was a weak reply. "No, of course not, I wouldn't—I mean, why would I want to do that?"

"So you could do what Eddie's doing. Saying he's had experience, saying he's grown up now, that he knows all about everything. Telling the same lies for the same reasons."

"I don't tell lies," Ben said. "When have I ever told you a lie?"

"Lies hurt, Ben," Jennie replied. "These lies could mark Gina for life. Don't you see that?"

Ben nodded hesitantly into his receiver. A dumb thing to do, he knew. But he couldn't think of anything to say that wasn't dumb.

64

Gina lay on top of her bed as her mother paced the small bedroom. She understood what her mother was feeling. Still, Gina had made her decision and wanted to stick with it. No matter how comforting it would have been to relent and tell.

"That's all you're going to say?" asked her mother.

"Mom, that's all I can say. I'm handling this."

"But what is it you're handling, Gina?" Her mother's voice rose with exasperation. "Sally Johnson felt she shouldn't tell me much of anything, only that there'd been an incident. Damn it, what incident?"

Gina shrugged but then sat up and looked directly at her mother. She hoped the message being sent sounded mature. "It's a boy-girl thing, Mom. It's nothing we haven't talked about before. Really."

"Gina, it's not like—it's not the same kind of thing that—"

"No," Gina lied. "It's way different. And I can handle it. Trust me."

"What choice do I have?" asked her mother.

"Someday I'll explain everything. I promise."

"When?"

"When this is all behind me. I promise."

Her mother did a complete, and despairing, three-sixty. As she opened her mouth to speak again, Gina leapt from her bed and ran to embrace her. "It'll all be fine, Mom. Don't worry."

Her mother smiled ruefully. "Hah!"

"I think I'll shower now and go to bed. O.K.?"

"O.K.?" replied her mother, but now with a sudden smile. "No, it isn't O.K. But I've got an idea. Why don't you shower now and go to bed?"

Gina nodded as her mother turned to head for the bedroom door.

After a few seconds of standing absolutely still in the center of her room, Gina began to undress.

She pulled on a robe, went into her bathroom, and closed the door behind her.

She turned on the shower taps and adjusted the heat of the water to bearable. She slipped off her robe and carefully stepped into the tub.

She stood motionlessly under the spray, her eyes closed, her hands at her sides. With a sudden energy that erupted within her, Gina began to scrub herself, every inch, every crevice, every strand of hair.

After a few minutes she was exhausted. She stood one moment more under the spray and then bent down to twist the taps. She reached out from behind the shower curtain and found a fresh towel and stood in the tub, drying off.

When she finally emerged from the shower, Gina felt slightly more relaxed and certainly cleaner.

She reached across the sink with a hand and cleared a space in the mirror to look at herself. She grinned at her reflection. Bedraggled but alive. She reached for the hair dryer.

She had wrapped her damp towel around herself

automatically, but as she turned this way and that to get her hair dry, the towel loosened. Gina let it fall.

She looked critically at herself in the mirror.

She laughed a little to herself. If her face wasn't enough to launch a thousand ships, her body was. Suddenly she remembered Jennie's comment on her first day at school, about how she, Gina, would be the envy of all the seventh graders and most of the eighth. She had a bosom. She had real woman's breasts. She had clear skin and an honest waist, and she was fairly tall. She knew her legs were good.

Objectively, after a moment, Gina decided she was what older people called a dish.

The thought amused her.

But only for a second as she became once more serious and thoughtful, although now with a difference. It was one thing having your mother tell you how pretty you were, how special, how talented. It was something else again to try to believe it.

Gina reddened a little with anger. At herself, first of all. She had a great body, damn it. And she wasn't dumb!

That son of a bitch Eddie Phipps should have his knees broken!

Gina's imagination took one more step down that path, but even to herself she couldn't think out loud what she really wanted.

There had to be something she could do!

She opened a drawer in the bathroom vanity table and pulled out a handful of cosmetics. In a kind of madness, Gina began applying mascara and eye shadow and lipstick.

She grabbed the hair dryer again and played a little with water and gel. She pulled her towel up off the bathroom floor and wrapped it around herself again, seductively this time.

Nearly breathless, Gina stood a moment looking at her reflection, smiling. She threw her shoulders back and thrust out her breasts.

Eat your heart out, world!

If only I had the guts, she told herself. If only, if only.

From the steam in the room, an idea emerged.

She stood, transfixed, as if listening to it.

There were four good reasons to pay attention.

The first had to do with Mac Love. She felt responsible for what might happen to him tomorrow.

The second had to do with Jennie. She knew Jennie would never be able to stay silent about what was going on. This would relieve her of her "medieval" vow.

The third had to do with Eddie Phipps. She knew that if she could do what was whirling in her mind, he would be destroyed.

And the fourth, the most important reason, had to do with herself. She felt she had taken one independent step. In order to keep walking unassisted, she had to take another.

She stood a moment without moving, staring into her own eyes in the mirror.

Yes, she said, I could do that. I could!

I could do it.

65

Bleary-eyed, Gina crawled out of bed and went into the bathroom. She snapped on the light over the mirror and gasped to see the smeared face that stared back at her. Then her ecstasy of planning from the night before swam back into her consciousness and, as she reached for cold-cream, she started to imagine her revenge all over again.

She thought about it as she showered and toweled off. But now it no longer seemed a sure thing.

The confidence she had felt only hours before was replaced by determination. She blow-dried her hair. Rather than make up her face as she had done in the first flush of plotting, she chose now instead to wear no cosmetics. And while she spent one moment standing straight and tall and looking at her figure in the mirror, she opted to dress down and slouch. She wasn't afraid of being seen as someone who had gotten exactly what she deserved. That image had given her a certain delight before bedtime the night before. But today she needed to be believed.

She dressed slowly, choosing sweater and jeans and shoes carefully, thinking all along. The one thing she didn't see herself doing was confiding in her teacher. The entire scene had to be sudden, unexpected, unstoppable. There was no way the woman, once clued in to what Gina wanted to do, would allow it. "No," she would say. "Let's go to the principal."

That was exactly what Gina didn't want. She felt that

the only satisfaction, and security, she could ever expect had to come from her own efforts. Anything "official" would perhaps make others feel better, but not Gina.

She chose not to eat anything for breakfast. She sipped orange juice and a little weak tea. Her mother, of course, noticed this, but said nothing.

Later, at the curb in front of school, she put the car in park and turned to Gina. "Are you going to tell me what's going on?"

"No," Gina replied as gently as she could.

Her mother sighed and put the car into gear. "You know, sweetheart, there isn't anything I wouldn't do to help you."

"I know."

"I love you, Gina. Don't do anything risky. Please."

Gina smiled a little. "It's not dangerous. At least, I don't think so."

Her mother nodded. "All right. I believe in you, Gina. I won't pry. I just hope you'll tell me all about this later."

Gina twisted in her seat, terribly nervous, and trying very hard not to show it. "If I can do this, Mom, I'll tell you. I promised you last night. If it doesn't work, well"—she shrugged—"I'll probably tell you that, too. Later. Some day."

66

Gina sat silently in her seat in homeroom. Jennie had tried to be sympathetic, to show concern, but Gina hadn't given her much time. Looking as composed as possible, she had marched determinedly up the steps into school and directly to her classroom. She took her seat in silence, Jennie nearby, and waited for the rest of the class to enter and quiet down.

Their homeroom teacher came in and walked to her desk. She stood at the front of the class and looked over the chairs, counting heads and identifying faces, and then bent down to register attendance in her log. When she straightened and looked as though she were about to speak, Gina raised her hand.

"Yes, Gina?"

Gina stood, in itself unusual. Her knees knocked, but she locked them into place, reminding herself that this was her only chance. It had to be done when Eddie Phipps was not in the same room. Oh, how she hoped she was right about all this!

Turning halfway around to face both the class and the teacher, Gina cleared her throat.

"I guess a lot of people think something—" and here, immediately, she stumbled. She couldn't imagine what words were suitable, even though she had practiced in her own mind since dressing. She would have to start again and just make a run for it.

"I guess a lot of people think something sexy happened last weekend," she stated more firmly.

She could feel attention focus.

"There are stories going around about how a boy in our class came to my house and had sex with me."

A rumble ran around the room.

"That isn't true," Gina said simply. "I wanted to tell you all what did happen."

Chairs creaked, and classmates shifted, leaning forward.

"Gina, I'm not sure this is the appropriate place to—" began her teacher. But without even looking at the woman, Gina raised her hand quickly, palm out. The teacher stopped.

"Last Saturday afternoon this boy came to my house. I made a mistake and let him in. I thought he was just sort of interested in me, wanted to be, well, nice to me."

Gina looked down at Jennie, who sat openmouthed. "He did, but he also had bigger plans.

"The story is that because this boy has a hickey, I did it with him. He has the 'evidence.' Well, I hope, I believe that now you all will have as much or more evidence as he."

Do it fast! she urged herself. "What happened"—she hurried on—"was this. He pinned me against the refrigerator and held my hands behind my back. He—he made his move. I asked him to stop, but he wouldn't."

She took a big breath. The beginning of tears formed in her eyes. She began to feel angry, not only at Eddie Phipps again but at herself for her weakness.

"He was kissing me, nuzzling. And all I could think to do, at first, was stand there, stupid, like a statue. But then I knew I had to do something else. So, I bit his neck. Hard. That's how he got his famous hickey!"

Her classmates murmured. Gina pressed on, determined and only now beginning to wonder whether she could, or should, use the words she heard in her mind.

"When I bit him, he backed away, a little. But it was enough. I kneed him, hard, in his—in his crotch. He finally backed off."

There was laughter in the room, not loud but genuine. Gina tried to smile in return, but she couldn't.

"I ran out of the house," she continued. "He came after me. I threatened to scream like crazy if he came at me. I guess he believed me. He got in his car and drove away, calling me a lot of names."

People looked at one another, questioning, believing, eager to leave the pressurized atmosphere of the classroom yet knowing they couldn't.

"So," Gina added, "I just wanted to put the record straight. This guy is going around saying I'm a certain kind of girl, and I'm not. I never have been. He says I'm hot and wild." Gina smiled finally, nearly finished. "I wouldn't know about that. But I do know that the hickey he's carrying around is a bite mark and that he's probably still a little sore between his legs."

At this the class erupted into laughter.

Gina sat down. She was breathless and shaking. Jennie reached over to put a hand on Gina's shoulder.

Gina shrugged Jennie off. After all, this was only Part One of her plan, the scene *she* could direct. She had no control over Part Two. That depended on other people.

She could only hope.

67

The conference between the Loves, the Phippses, and the school principal had been scheduled during first lunch.

It didn't take place.

When Mrs. Phipps arrived at school, she found Eddie outside, waiting for her.

"Let's just get out of here," Eddie said in a hurry, jumping into the passenger seat of the Mercedes.

"Edward, what's wrong? We have to get to the principal. I want to know what happened yesterday, and why, and I want that boy punished."

"It doesn't matter," Eddie said hotly. "Let's just get out of here."

"Edward, that would be running away. That boy deserves to be suspended or expelled. At least he has to explain his behavior."

"Mother, believe me, I really want to go away to school. Now. I don't want to disappoint you or Dad. I'm ready. Let's just go, please!"

Mrs. Phipps looked at her son skeptically, not understanding that in his mind he was hearing laughter and jokes and disdain.

And Eddie, turned away from her and staring out the window at the emptied front lawn of his school, swallowed hard, trying to understand what had gone wrong.

A station wagon drew up behind the Mercedes. From it emerged Mac Love's parents.

Eddie heard the car doors close nearby. He looked over his shoulder. "Will you just get this heap out of here!" he shouted at his mother.

68

It wasn't only Eddie Phipps who disappeared at first lunch.

Gina had been escorted to the principal's office by her homeroom teacher. She had stood silently by while her teacher reported the early-morning scene.

"Is that all true?" he had asked Gina.

"Yes."

The principal looked at her for a moment in silence. "I'm sorry to hear this, but I'm very glad you did what you did. Now, Gina, it's up to the school to handle things."

"What do you mean?"

"Well, we—the faculty that is—may find that Eddie Phipps is not the sort of young man we want here on campus."

Snap! Part Two! Gina waited, not daring to hope.

"How are you feeling?" the principal asked then, surprising Gina with his concern. "Would you like to call your mother?"

"I don't know," Gina answered. And then she did know how she was feeling. She should have felt proud and triumphant. She realized suddenly she felt exhausted, empty, wasted. "I guess I'm a little shaky," she admitted after a moment.

"I'm not surprised," said the principal. "Maybe you could use a day off. What do you think?"

Gina looked up at the principal. She really couldn't speak. Her eyes did. She tried to shrug and wipe at them at the same time.

"Maybe I could," she said finally.

69

"I don't know whether I could have done it," Jennie said to Ben during lunch hour.

"It was amazing," Ben agreed.

Jennie put her hot dog down on her plate and wiped her hands. "Would you do that to me?" she asked.

"Do what?"

"Try to . . . you know."

"Oh, come on! We talked about this!"

"I'm serious. Would you? I mean, suppose you thought that was what I wanted. Would you just force yourself on me?"

Ben knew he was about to fall into a muddy hole. Slippery. One false word and he would never be able to get out. He wiped his mouth and coughed.

"Well?" Jennie persisted.

"No."

"Really?"

"I wouldn't," Ben said, trying to look serious. Suddenly he recalled what his father had said. "Because if both people aren't . . . well, in love, I guess . . . it doesn't really have any . . . warmth."

"Warmth?" Jennie smiled at the word.

Ben looked at his plate.

"You know, I always thought Eddie was a creep. I understand bragging and all, but he's just so mean!"

Ben nodded uncomfortably. He still sensed the slippery walls staring up at him. Better just to let Jennie run on.

"I mean, you guys just don't think."

Ben shrugged. What would Felix shoot back?

Jennie reddened a little. "I don't mean you, Ben. Just guys in general."

The hole began to fill of its own accord. Ben finished his hot dog.

70

Gina was grateful for her mother's gentleness. She knew the tangle of emotions her mother must have felt.

Having been summoned from work by the principal's call, Gina's mother had driven them both home. She had tried neither to smother Gina with affection and comfort, nor to grill her for more details than were available in the principal's office. While she felt dismayed her daughter hadn't confided in her, she also was proud Gina had faced down her devils independently.

Gina sensed all this. It gave her pleasure and a feeling of relief.

After she had been put tenderly to bed, and her mother had driven back to the hospital, Gina fell into a troubled sleep. When she awoke a few hours later, she was surprised to find out where she was and then to remember why.

She stood and walked to her window. The sun shone brilliantly. Through the open window Gina could hear the sea.

She stood a moment, transfixed by the sound. The ocean today was aroar with surf crashing on the rocks and shoreline. She looked at the trees outside her window, but there was no real wind. She smiled suddenly. The ocean was applauding her, cheering for her.

She turned and walked into the bathroom. She snapped on its light and looked at herself in the mirror over the sink. She couldn't help herself and felt foolish even as she began to laugh at her reflection. She had a sudden urge to high-five her image. Instead, she stood in the small room, bouncing up and down. "Yes!" she whispered happily. "Yes!"

A telephone rang in the living room.

Gina turned quickly and ran to answer it.

"Gina? Are you all right?"

Gina recognized the voice.

"I am. I'm terrific!"

There was a pause on the line.

"That's what I thought, too. I just wanted you to know," MacNulty Love said.